With a slight pressure, he turned her around and captured her lips with his. As she touched his waist, attempting to gain access to his manhood, his hands grasped hers intertwining their fingers. "Not enough time," he whispered. A vacuum of pressure seemed to pull him backward, "Find me." These final words were spoken as the wind picked up once more and the night enclosed them in nothingness.

****

An Introduction to the
Moon Magick Series

Welcome Dear Readers,

   I invite you into a world of magick. Here you will meet a family of powerful women who practice the New Orleans form of witchcraft.

   You'll meet Arabella, who finds herself drawn to a beautiful man in her dreams; only to find that he's lying in a hospital bed, hopelessly paralyzed.

   Love is the greatest power in this story - you'll see it heal the hopeless, bridge the chasms of prejudice, and ignite passions that burn as brightly as the stars.

   I hope you enjoy Arabella and Jade - they effectively prove the point - love can conquer all.

'Josie Arlington'

"A Wishing Moon"

By

Josie Arlington

Baby, Thanks for reading my work. I hope you enjoy

This is a work of fiction. Names, characters, places and incidents are either the product of the author's imagination or used fictitiously, and any resemblance to actual persons, living or dead, business establishments, events or locales is entirely coincidental.

"A Wishing Moon"

All rights reserved
Copyright - 2010 - *Josie Arlington*

Thank You

Tracy - for your technical expertise and invaluable help
Frances - for your unique perspective and ability to see a hole in the plot a mile away
Jarrod - for just being you and for posing for the cover
Mary – Thanks for being beautiful – on the cover and off

I would like to credit Silver Ravenwolf and her writings for inspiration as well as for the phrase *I am the flow and I am the ebb, I am the weaver and I am the web.*
I have borrowed that phrase in my own hoodoo work as well as including it in my character's spell work.

She uses this phrase in all of her books - she may not have been the originator – but just in case – I will give her credit.

~ Prologue ~

The kiss was feathery light, with just the tip of his tongue parting her lips. She breathed in his scent; he smelled of warm sunshine and salt spray. The palms of her hands moved feverishly over his golden skin, up over his broad shoulders and around his strong neck. His hair was quite long and the color of sunflower honey. Her fingers clutched the long strands at the back of his neck. She fought the urge to wrap one leg around his hip in a soundless plea to be filled. A desperate hunger made her tingle and yearn.

Joy coursed through her bloodstream as he cupped her hips in his hands, first pulling her up hard against him and then picking her up from the ground. Gratefully, her legs parted and she encircled his waist, pressing her soft center up against his rough jeans. Racing uncontrollably, her heart felt as if it were going to burst through her chest. His lips caressed her mouth and then wandered across her jaw and down the side of her neck. She gasped with passion, never had she felt so molten and eager. Arching her back, she met his gaze. Eyes the color of a tiger's eye jewel, framed with thick dark lashes, feasted on her face. "Who are you?" she gasped.

Instead of the answer she longed for, he bent low and warmly nuzzled the top of one of her breasts. The gentle swell peeked from the top of the silk nightgown that clung damply to her fevered body. Muscles in her thighs contracted and her hips longed to thrust forward against him.

There was delightful stubble on his chin that chafed her skin and Arabella reveled in the slight pain the friction generated. "Please . . ." she breathed. Allowing one hand to support her weight, he slid the other hand between their bodies and gently palmed the silk and lace that provided a filmy barrier to paradise. Sensing no resistance, he pressed on, pushing the delicate material aside and slipping his strong fingers deep inside her.

Light and heat exploded within her and she threw back her head and screamed. As she convulsed in ecstasy, he pressed gentle lips to her ear and whispered, "Come to me." The last thing she saw before reality dimmed was a full wishing moon shining bright in the velvet sky.

❰ * ~ Chapter I ~ * ❱

Arabella lifted her hips off of the bed, vainly searching for someone that wasn't there. Quaking with desire, she wrapped her arms around herself and tried to breathe. She lay back for a moment and just relished the sensations. Never had she experienced a dream so intense, yet the climax that was still vibrating between her legs was definitely real.

Searching her memory, she relived the dream. Who was he? It seemed as if she should know him, but for the life of her she could not remember where she would have known him from. Maybe, the familiarity was just an aftereffect of the incredibly erotic dream. A face and a body like his would have been impossible to forget. She closed her eyes and fought to hold on to the memory of his touch, to the look in his eyes. Waking to find it had all been a dream was sheer torture. Every fiber in her being made her want to reach out and take him in her arms once again.

Frustrating.

Maybe it was time for her to find a real lover.

She flung the sheet off of her body and sat up on the side of the bed. Slowly she stood, and steadied herself enough to walk to the bathroom. Pulling the silk gown over her head, she turned on the shower and faced herself in the vanity mirror. Lifting her long dark hair from her neck, she twisted it into a knot and secured it with a clip. Leaning closer to the mirror, she gasped. Flipping on the brighter overhead light, she could not believe her eyes or her fingers. Dream or no dream, her neck and upper chest were covered with a faint red rash; a rash that had been left by her dream lover's five o' clock shadow.

The abrasions on her soft skin seemed to be evidence that more had happened in the twilight hours than just a dream. This intrigued Arabella. How was this possible? Could he be a real person? Could she return to his arms?

The possibilities that raced through her mind would have been unusual for most people, but Arabella Landry was not your typical twenty-four year old woman.

Arabella looked at life through different eyes. For her, the world was a magical place, where probability and certainty could be manipulated by sheer will, and forces that existed beyond the bounds of the imagination could be tapped into and used to create reality. That was the way that she had been brought up; she accepted magick as a way of life.

When she viewed last night's dream through the lens of magick, a whole new world of possibilities opened up. Something within her was convinced that the Adonis with the incredible body was a real, flesh and blood man. Arabella wanted to believe that with everything that was in her.

He had to be real. His words to her were burned in her memory. "Come to me,' he had said. And that was exactly what she intended to do . . . just as soon as she figured out how. She made the shower a quick one. And after drying herself off with a towel, she slipped on jeans and a soft cotton top.

From the mirror, she could see the reflection of her bed. Nothing would have made her happier than to crawl back between its soft, welcoming sheets and dream. She wanted to see him again. She wrapped her arms around herself and remembered what it was like to cling to that chest and those shoulders which were as broad as a bus. And that face! He had the face of an angel. Undeniably, he was the most powerfully built man she could ever remember seeing, or touching, or kissing.

Arabella did not have a lot of experience with men. It had always been difficult for her to open up to people, so often when she tried, she had been slapped down for her trouble. So far, she hadn't been lucky enough to find a man who could accept her for what she was. Last night there had been no judgment in his eyes, only acceptance and desire.

She wanted to hold on to every detail of last night's

dream. The desperation to do something to connect with the sexy phantasm bedeviled her and suddenly she realized that she must make a sketch of him before a single detail of his beautiful face faded from her memory. She sped down the stairs and found her sketch book.

Flipping the switch on the coffee pot, she hopped up on one of the bar stools and began to draw . . . *him*. High cheekbones, chiseled features, soft hair, well defined abs and steel-strong legs all added up to much more than a sum of the parts. The smoldering look that she added to his face came straight from her mind's eye. She ran her right hand over the drawing, remembering how it had felt to run her hand over his skin.

Propping the sketchpad up on the bar, she poured herself a cup of strong, fragrant coffee. Adding sugar and cream, she stirred the mixture and then licked the spoon, all the while studying the portrait that she had quickly drawn. He still looked vaguely familiar.

A sense of urgency washed over her. How could she just go about the tasks of the day after last night's experience? How could she think of anything else but him?

****

Jade Landale was a prisoner in his own body. Just a few weeks ago, he had been vibrant and alive and free. Now, he might as well be dead - in fact he was beginning to wish that he was. Paralyzed from his neck down, he could not even swallow on his own. Communication was impossible. Reese had tried, he had kept asking him questions and instructing him to blink if he understood, but the doctors were not the least bit encouraging. They kept using the term - catastrophic injury. Apparently, this time he had really gone and done it. Kate had been after him to give up the extreme sports that he loved so well, she said that his career was more important, but he loved the feeling of scaling a sheer rock wall or free diving in the depths of the sea. She had told him he was going to kill himself, and it looks like she had been right.

Since the diagnosis, Kate had only been in to see him twice and the last time she was here, Jade knew that she had given up on him. She could not even bring herself to touch his hand. His girlfriend had always been overly squeamish. Apparently, it was more than she could stomach to have a fiancé who was no better than a vegetable. Despite what Reese had told her about the blinking, Kate did not believe that he could hear her or understand her. Frankly, it was hard to transmit a message to someone who wouldn't look you in the eyes.

Dr. Reynolds did not want to give up on him; he had said that more tests needed to be done before they could be positive of Jade's prognosis. One of the other doctors that was assisting on his case said that he wasn't even sure that Jade had any cognizant awareness of his surroundings at all, but he did – much to his dismay, he was aware of everything.

The realization of his situation terrified Jade. He screamed endlessly in his head. Over and over, he relived the moment when the bolt failed and he had fallen from one of the sheer faces of E-Rock. He had known from the moment he had landed so brutally and awkwardly at the base of the cliff that it was bad. Blessedly, he had only remained conscious for a few moments before passing out. From the moment he had regained consciousness, he had known something was horribly wrong, because he had felt nothing - absolutely nothing.

The only relief he seemed to have was his dreams. In his dreams, he could walk and talk and hope and believe that somehow this nightmare would soon be over. Reese and other members of his staff still refused to believe that it was all over. After all, they had pinned their hopes on him being the next Governor of the grand state of Texas. Now, it would seem as if that particular dream was over.

While a nurse turned him from side to side, giving him a sponge bath, he escaped to a better place deep within his own mind. Last night, he had experienced a particularly intense and strange dream. He had been back on Enchanted Rock – not climbing this time, but with a woman – an amazingly beautiful woman. His dream body had reacted instantly to her, and without the expectations of reality, he had enjoyed her in ways that he knew he would probably never enjoy a woman again. She had been so lovely and so very responsive.

It seemed that dreams were his only solace, now. He much preferred that alternate reality to this one. It reminded him of something his great grandmother used to tell him. The only daughter of a Cherokee medicine man, she had carried with her the old ways and the old beliefs. She used to tell him that even though her body was stiff and uncooperative, that at night – in her dreams – she went to places that she could not go and did things that she was no longer capable of doing. She had called it 'walking on the wind'. Maybe, that's what he had been doing. One thing he knew, it sure beat the hell out of where he was now. He shut his eyes and left the room.

****

'What a shame! What a waste!' Nurse Eddings washed the perfect body of the young man who was now no more than a pliable statue. She had seen several people in nearly the same shape that he was in, but he was the worst that she had ever had the misfortune to be around. There was no coming back from this type of accident. This man was completely paralyzed from his brain stem, south.

The doctors had said that any remaining brain function was questionable, but she could see the panic and despair in his eyes and she knew that he fully understood the utter hopelessness of his situation. And what a bright future he had left behind. How terribly, terribly sad.

****

A plan began to formulate in Arabella's mind, things that her mother and grandmother had taught her. Quickly she grabbed a pad and pen and made a list of items that she could use to insure that she returned to the dream state where she left him. Hastily, she wrote:

Mugwort
Lavender
Amethyst gemstone
Purple mojo bag
Purple candle

Everything in her longed to get started *now*, but going back to bed immediately after rising wouldn't accomplish the rest of the day's work. With reluctance, she laid aside the note until later in the day and reached for her date book. Arabella kept an extensive journal where she wrote everything down. She flipped open the book that was part almanac, part Book of Shadows and part a daily to-do list.

Since graduating from the University of Texas with a degree in computer science, she had built a successful home business for herself. Combining her green thumb, her magical acumen and considerable computer skills, she had founded *Wildflower Way*. Her brain child was a company that sold dried herbs, oils, tinctures and herbal formulas that she created for a number of health issues such as rheumatism, allergies, low energy and headaches. Her home in the Texas Hill Country was an oasis of lush gardens, greenhouses and enchanted paths that connected small rustic buildings where she dried herbs and flowers and concocted the potions that she packaged and shipped to satisfied customers across the country. Arabella was proud of her gardens and many people stopped just to look in amazement at the varied plantings that she maintained. Some would ask what her secret was; she had no answer for them. She could hardly tell them her mother's explanation – that the garden of a good witch always flourishes. Sketching and drawing were also passions of hers and she designed a catalogue, labels and seed packets to complement the products that *Wildflower Way* offered to the consumer.

Glancing at the entry for today, she reminded herself that this was a special holiday. December 21st – the winter solstice. It was a sacred time when candles were lit and future plans were made. Tonight, her grandmother Nanette Beaureguarde would scry the future. It was something she did on this, one of the most magical nights on the wheel of the year. All of the family knew that they would hear from her if she saw anything of interest, but in the meantime, Arabella had Yule preparations to make. The whole Beaureguarde clan was coming to her house for the holidays, so there was baking, shopping and decorating to be done.

Wildflower Way was a special place during each of the seasons, and winter was no exception. Today was also Sunday, so she was free to do exactly what she pleased, any orders that had to be filled could wait for the next day.

Once again, her hand moved to her neck to linger on the light abrasions that were still present, the small bumps were the only real link that she possessed to the incredibly intriguing man that haunted her every thought. 'Stop!' she chided herself, 'that will just have to wait until later'. She stepped over to her recipe file to pull a few holiday favorites. A trip to the organic food market in neighboring Austin was next on her agenda.

The abrupt ringing of the telephone interrupted her musings. She leaned over and picked up the phone and was met with sobs on the other end.

"Hello, this is Arabella Landry, may I help you?" Arabella had known this would not be a customer, as this was her private line.

"Arabella, something terrible has happened." At first, she did not recognize the voice, but then the face of a neighbor came to her mind - it was Rachel Townsend.

"What's wrong, Rachel?"

"Kathy and Lea are gone – they're just gone."

Rachel Townsend, her daughter Kathy and granddaughter Lea lived about a half mile down the road that led south to Wimberley. Although, Arabella had known Rachel for years, they were not close.

"Tell me everything," she urged the distraught woman.

"May I come over, please?"

"Certainly, I will be waiting for you." 'What was going on?' she wondered to herself. In times like this, she wished that she possessed her mother's gift of second sight. Elizabeth was known to be able to pull information from out of the ether – especially things that pertained to her daughter. Her mother's ability had plagued Arabella during her teenage years, making it nearly impossible for her to hide anything from her parent. The older she got, the more she realized it wasn't always a bad thing – being connected to someone else like that.

Rachel Townsend knew firsthand that Arabella had gifts of her own. At one time Arabella and Kathy had been friends, until Rachel had forced Kathy to abandon their friendship because she felt that Arabella's beliefs were evil and dangerous. So, based on their history, Arabella knew that Rachel Townsend considered her situation to be desperate – or she would never have resorted to contacting the likes of Arabella Landry.

Before her guest arrived, Arabella straightened a few things and set out another mug and some Morning Glory muffins that she had made the day before. Southern hospitality was ingrained in Arabella's very soul. Rachel did not have far to come, so she arrived a few moments later.

Arabella met her at the front door and escorted the shaking woman to a comfortable seat in the living room. She was a tall, lanky woman with perfectly coiffed brown hair. Rachel grasped Arabella's hands and looked her straight in the eye. "Something has happened to my child and my granddaughter, I just know it."

"When was the last time that you saw them?" Arabella searched Rachel's face for an ulterior motive, but saw only grief. She hated to be suspicious of the woman, but Rachel Townsend had dealt Arabella a great deal of misery in years past.

"I saw them before I went to work yesterday morning." Rachel Townsend was a real estate agent in Wimberley. Although the nations housing market was suffering, the area around Austin was somewhat immune, college towns usually were. Nevertheless, Rachel was a very successful business woman.

"Did you talk to her during the day?" Arabella knew that Kathy had made the hard decision to live with her mother after a rather messy divorce and had been staying at home with her five year old daughter.

"She phoned me about ten o' clock yesterday morning to tell me that she and Lea were going out to look for

Pumpkin, Lea's little white poodle. I let the dog out for a bathroom run yesterday morning, and before I left I called and called ... but the dog didn't show up. You haven't seen him, have you?"

"No, I haven't seen Pumpkin, but I'll keep an eye out for him. Have you notified the police yet?" Arabella thought she knew the answer to this question, but she asked it anyway. She poured the pale woman a cup of coffee and motioned toward the sugar and cream.

"I called them, but not enough time has passed. Officer Myers said that I have to wait at least twenty four hours before filing a missing persons report. Also, since Kathy is an adult, they have to consider that she just picked up Lea and left. Arabella, I know something is wrong. I can feel it." Sympathy welled up in Arabella and the former reticence that she had felt melted away. She put her arm around Rachel and hugged her. Rachel Townsend broke down and cried.

Not wanting to assume anything, especially considering their volatile history, Arabella carefully asked. "How can I help, Rachel?"

Rachel straightened herself and wiped her eyes with a crisp cotton handkerchief that she drew from her Dooney and Bourke bag. "I want you to do what you do – I want you to find Kathy and Lea."

"Did you bring anything with you that they have recently touched or something that was special to them?" Rachel reached into her purse and began taking out items. Arabella realized that Rachel remembered what she had seen a much younger Arabella do at the birthday sleepover nearly ten years ago. As a form of entertainment, Arabella had taken turns reading items that the other girls had given her and she had told them things that she couldn't possibly have known. This had thrilled and mystified the girls, but it had horrified Rachel Townsend and she had sent a humiliated and embarrassed Arabella home right in the middle of the party.

Rachel handed her a pair of sunglasses and a toy mermaid: a small *Ariel* doll that had seen much wear at the hands of a little girl. Slowly, Arabella reached out her hand to accept the pitiful offerings. First the sunglasses; Arabella ran her fingers over the rims and lingered longer on the pieces that fit over the ear and the part that set over the bridge of the nose. These were the parts that came into greater contact with Kathy's face and carried the most lingering vibrations. As she touched the glasses, she closed her eyes and tuned into the connection that bound Kathy McLemore with something that she wore every day. A warm sensation began to flow from the object into Arabella's hands. As always, with her eyes closed Arabella began to see images and she also started to experience emotions that she had no reason to feel. Waves of fear and panic began to seize Arabella and she saw Kathy shout at the little girl to 'Run, Lea, Run!' Rough hands threw Kathy to the ground and a sudden blow to the head sent the whole vision into blackness.

    Waiting a few moments and trying to get her blood pressure back to normal; Arabella took a few deep breaths. She knew that Rachel was literally sitting on the edge of her seat, waiting to hear what Arabella had seen. She dreaded telling her the truth, but the truth was all that she had. "I saw Kathy tell Lea to run and I felt big, rough hands grab and strike Kathy down. Rachel, Kathy and Lea were first attacked in your kitchen."

    Rachel Townsend looked flabbergasted, "There were absolutely no signs of a struggle, not a thing was out of place." Her tone did not infer that she did not believe Arabella, only that she was trying to make sense out of what she was hearing.

    "Apparently, someone set everything back into order." Arabella tried to help Rachel with an explanation. "How about Kathy's purse and keys, were those left behind?"

    "No, all of that was gone. That was the first thing the police asked me and probably the reason that they told me she had most likely left of her own free will." Rachel held out the small doll and Arabella took it, dreading this part the most of all.

    She held the doll and touched it the way a small child

would, holding it tightly to her breast and reaching down and touching the head and hair of the doll with her face.

Confusion and terror washed over Arabella and the vision that came to her eyes was the back yard of Rachel's house. Lea was running from someone and out of nowhere a hand snatched her off the ground and she felt Lea's small legs and arms flailing against her attacker. She felt her mouth being covered by a large rough palm and the air flow into her nose was being blocked. Arabella choked and coughed and sadly laid the loved, worn doll down on the table. "Lea was taken, also. I can tell it is a large man, I received no glimpse of his face, but his hands were unusually rough and calloused."

"Oh, this is terrible," Rachel wailed. "I was so hoping that the police were right, but I knew in my heart that Kathy and Lea had not left without telling me. We had not had any serious disagreements, they were not unhappy and we were making plans for Christmas. Kathy and I had already bought toys for Lea and they are still in the closet waiting to be wrapped – I checked. I knew that if Kathy had gone with someone willingly, she would not have left Lea's Christmas presents behind." Despair made Rachel's head too heavy to hold up. She slumped over and buried her face into the palms of her hands. "Is there anything else you can do, any more that you can tell me?"

Arabella thought for a moment about what would be best. "I can use my pendulum and check a map of the area to see if I can tell which way they were taken."

"Yes, yes," Rachel grasped on to any glimmer of hope. "Look at the map" Arabella got up and found her crystal quartz pendulum that hung on a simple silver chain. In a desk drawer she found a map of the Texas Hill country and she spread it out on the coffee table, then sat down in front of it and held the pendulum over the area as near to the Townsend home as she possibly could. She could clearly see Cypress Creek and Ranch Road 12, and so that was where she centered the pendulum. Usually, the pointed piece of crystal would slowly begin to move and gradually it would swing more and more toward the area in question.

This time, however, the pendulum refused to move an iota. Rather, it stood stock still except for a peculiar downward pulling sensation. A thought entered Arabella's mind, "Rachel, I don't think Kathy and Lea ever left your property. Is there some place that they could be hiding?"

❰* ~ Chapter II ~ *❱

The winter solstice had arrived in New Orleans, bringing a slightly cooler temperature of 52 degrees. Nanette Beaureguarde shuffled around the dining room table gathering the tools that she would need to peer into the future. Each December 21st, she filled a cauldron with water strictly for the purpose of gazing into its inky depths to see what she could see. The murky water came from an old well that was dug by slaves on a plantation in New Iberia parish on Bayou Teche. Many was the time that area girls would gaze down into the dark waters on the night of a full moon to see if they would behold the face of their future husband. One bright moonlit night in 1956, Nanette Robicheaux had clearly seen the face of Alcee Beaureguarde. "Angelique! Angelique!" She called her companion of twenty five years. "I'm ready to scry!"

The two women were inseparable. Angelique didn't just work for the family, she was family. She also shared Nanette's magical way of life. The two ladies practiced witchcraft, or their version of it. In New Orleans, traditional witchcraft is a combination of the Celtic craft, voodoo, hoodoo, with a little Appalachian Granny Magic thrown in for good measure. If you asked them what their religion was, they would tell you Catholic. Their everyday life, however, was filled with mojo bags, spells, charms and a constant awareness of the supernatural.

Angelique came into the room. She was a few years younger than Nanette and quite a few pounds lighter. Her skin tone was the color of coffee that had been sweetened by a few dollops of rich cream. "I have the mugwort and the sea salt," she announced to Nanette. "The black cord, the crystals and the candles are in the bottom drawer of the buffet cabinet."

Nanette opened the drawer and withdrew the contents that she needed. She sat down heavily in one of the straight back chairs. Angelique placed the cauldron in front of her and filled it with the fresh water. She arranged the black cord in a circle around the cauldron and then sprinkled the mugwort within the circle. "Mugwort will power the spell." Nanette held her hands, palm upward and closed her eyes. Angelique sat beside her and watched her work.

Even though Angelique's background was Santeria, she deferred to Nanette who came from a long line of powerful women. Nanette began by calling the quarters, "Guardians of the East, element of Air, hear my plea. Guardians of the West, element of Water, hear my request. Guardians of the South, element of Fire, I ask of thee a boon. Guardians of the North, element of Earth, hear my voice." Angelique handed her a white candle and a bottle of psychic power oil made from magnolia leaves. She dressed the white candle with the oil by taking the oil on the tip of her finger and rubbing it down the candle from the wick to the base. She lit the candle and then in turn lit a yellow, a blue, a red, and a green candle with the flame of the white candle. She picked up a large amethyst crystal and held it in her right hand and then she began to speak.

"Water, black as the night.

Grant me the gift of second sight.

Let me see my loved ones dear.

To me reveal their future clear."

She dipped the crystal in the water and then touched it to the center of her forehead. She laid the crystal down and began to gaze into the water.

Several moments passed. Angelique edged closer, but not too close. She did not want to interfere. Finally, Nanette began to speak, "I see much happiness at **Wildflower Way**. Love will come calling this year." Nanette leaned over and looked even deeper into the depths of the cauldron. Suddenly she reached out and grasped Angelique's hand.

Angelique knew the signs. Nanette had seen something bad. She had sat here by her when Nanette had seen death coming. She had lived with her through the loss of Nanette's husband Alcee and their daughter Aimee. She could feel the heat leaving Nanette's hand as a cold chill covered her body. "I see trouble. I see pain. I see death."

"Can you tell who?" Angelique whispered.

"No, but I am not letting this happen again." The older woman's voice was trembling. "Call Evangeline and pack our bags. We're going to Texas earlier that we planned and we're staying as long as it takes."

****

Evangeline led the tour group back into the Bayou Magick shop that was owned by her boss, Cherline Sonnier. The shop was not a tourist trap, but actually sold supplies for those who practiced real magick. That did not keep tourists from coming; in fact the selection of genuine ingredients such as herbs, gemstones, oils, and incenses fascinated them. In addition, real practitioners frequented the store and this was an additional draw to those who came to the Big Easy for a taste of the exotic and the mysterious. Cherline had taken advantage of this interest and started a tour of New Orleans that focused on the city's magical legacy.

A shy teenage girl with glasses and braces managed to edge her way to the front of the others and ask in a low tone, "Are you a real witch?" Evangeline sensed a longing for acceptance and empowerment in the young girl's words. She wished that she had time to spend with the lonely young woman. Evangeline just knew things about people after only a few moments. By meeting the eyes of this girl, she saw parents who were divorced, an unrequited love with the boy next door and an intense longing to feel in control of her life.

"Yes, I am." Evangeline answered. "Witch is not the only term that my family uses, we also call ourselves rootworkers."

Another tourist spoke up, interested in the exchange, "What's the difference between a rootworker and a witch?"

Evangeline probably answered this question at least once a night on the magic tours. The idea of someone who could really perform magic was intoxicating to most people.

"A rootworker's background is mainly hoodoo which is not a religion like Wicca, but true American folk magic. I am a witch; not because I belong to a coven, but because I was born one." She showed the group of twelve gris-gris bags, voodoo poppets, crystals and amulets specifically designed to draw love, money or give the wearer protection from their enemies.

Evangeline pushed her long dark hair off her shoulders. The long black dress and floor length cape that she wore was a costume, but she didn't mind wearing it at all. Her eyes were Creole black, actually the darkest navy blue, and her skin was a light olive. She was tall, beautiful and carried herself proudly. After checking out the customers who had chosen to purchase a few magical items, Evangeline consulted the schedule to see when the next tour group would show up.

The *Walk of Magic* was a two hour tour that carried the group from the Voodoo Museum on Dumaine, to the tomb of Marie Laveau at St Louis Cemetery #1, to Congo Square in the Louis Armstrong Park with many other interesting stops along the way.

Evangeline had been working for Cherline full time since she graduated high school and part time since she turned sixteen. Full time for Evangeline was the night tours, a schedule she could easily handle and still maintain her full class load at Tulane. Nanette had been pushing her to stay the full four years at Tulane, but what she really wanted to do was to go the University of Texas and live near her first cousin Arabella, whom she adored. From what she had read, Austin was one of the few places in the south that would be as accepting of her chosen lifestyle as New Orleans had been.

The curtain to the back room shifted and Cherline emerged. "Nanette said for you to come home; that it was urgent."

"Is she ill?" Evangeline reached under the counter for her purse.

"No, but she said that you all were going to Texas for a few weeks, at least. She asked for a leave of absence for you."

"Is that going to be all right with you?" Evangeline had no doubt that Cherline had at least three other girls all anxious to step into her shoes. Regardless, she did not want to burn any bridges or hurt Cherline's feelings.

"Of course," Cherline knew that while the other girls might be adequate tour guides, they would not have the intimate knowledge of the topic that Evangeline possessed. That knowledge, as the television commercial professed, was priceless. "Nanette seemed to be upset. I hope nothing is wrong." Cherline walked Evangeline to the door of the shop.

"I'm sure we can handle it, whatever it is – but thanks." Evangeline hurried to her car which was parked in a public garage a few blocks away. An uneasy feeling was flooding her body. What had she done? Two weeks ago she had begun a seven day ritual using small seeds called Job's tears. She had prayed over them, asking to be allowed to move to Austin. Nanette had been adamantly against her leaving New Orleans for any longer than just a few days. Evangeline was all Nanette had left of her beloved daughter, Aimee.

For seven days she had carried the seeds in a red flannel bag next to her heart. At the end of the week she had taken them down to the bridge and thrown them over her left shoulder into the Mississippi. She had stood there and recited the 23rd Psalm and then walked away without looking back. This was the seventh night since the culmination of the ritual and now the answer had come. She was heading to Texas for more than a few days, but at what cost?

****

Arabella had taken care of Rachel as best she could. She had made meticulous notes of all the information that she had managed to garner from her readings. Rachel wanted her to come over to her house and see if she could pick anything else up, but Arabella had insisted that she have the police investigate first. If the house and yard was truly a crime scene, she surely did not want to be the one that contaminated or obliterated crucial evidence. Rachel had said that she understood and she had gone home alone - lonely and scared. There wasn't too many more hours before the police would consider the situation more seriously and come onto the property and see what they could find. After they had done what they could, then Arabella would be glad to go over and help out in any way that she could. She knew from experience, however, that not many on the police force welcomed the type of help that she could provide - so the longer she could stay in the background the better.

Knowing that she had done all she could, Arabella turned her attention to more pleasant things. The day had been eaten up by Rachel Townsend's sadness and the rest of the time she had spent in Austin buying the supplies that she would need for her cooking and baking. Last minute gifts were purchased and Arabella had also gone by the University Co-op and picked up some T-shirts and a backpack that sported the Longhorn emblem for her cousin Evangeline. Angelique, Nanette's companion, would be coming, as well as Arabella's mother Elizabeth.

Arabella's father, Thomas Landry, had been gone for over five years now – the victim of an off-shore, oil rig accident. Not a day past that she did not recall his kind face and his loving smile. Elizabeth's and her families' powers had not scared Thomas. He had been confident enough in his own strength to view their unique abilities as something to cherish and protect instead of fear and avoid. Not all men were like that, Arabella knew this from experience. She missed her father.

Arabella's mother, Elizabeth, was still young, vital, and extremely attractive. She was very happily settled in Galveston, Texas. Right now, she was spending every spare moment cleaning up and rebuilding her beautiful home that had been devastated by Hurricane Ike. Storms had dealt harsh blows to their families, Ike had taken Elizabeth's home, but Katrina had taken Arabella's grandfather Alcee and Evangeline's mother Aimee. It had been almost four years, but the pain was still fresh enough to bring Nanette to her knees. She had seen a great flood in the scrying waters on Winter Solstice of 2003 but after almost a year past with nothing bad happening, Nanette had let her guard down. Then Katrina came. Surprisingly, the great hurricane had passed without completely devastating New Orleans, but then the levees had failed and the floods rose quickly with deadly results. All that year, Nanette had kept Alcee and Aimee away from Ponchatrain and away from the river, but the black waters had flowed down their own street and caught them by surprise.

Fighting back unpleasant memories, Arabella turned her mind to the sweet prospect of reuniting with her dream lover. It was almost time to go to bed and Arabella had prepared for it as if she were preparing for a date, or more truthfully, a romantic interlude. She had bathed in scented water and pampered her body with lotions and creams. She had constructed a dream pillow of purple cotton and filled it with lavender and mugwort. Mugwort, known as the witch's herb, was not only in the dream pillow; she had also used it to make smudge sticks and walked about her bedroom letting the smoke fill every nook and cranny. Two bundles of lavender hung from the bed posts and she had drunk a cup of tea made from the same two herbs. Angelique had taught her that if you don't usually dream, mugwort will help you dream. If you can't remember your dreams, the herb will allow you to recall more details than you normally would. People that usually remember their dreams can also use mugwort to dream consciously, in other words to be able to control your actions while dreaming. The latter was Arabella's intent; she wanted her dream to be as real as possible.

Despite all of the work that she had put into her dream time, sleep was a long time coming. The events of the day had been unsettling. The disappearance of Kathy McLemore and her daughter had put a damper on Arabella's spirits and the whole atmosphere of her usually happy home.

Arabella lay restlessly, attempting every trick she could remember to hurry the onset of sleep. The more anxious she became, however, the more elusive sleep proved to be. Finally, she gave in and turned on the light and reached for a book. Maybe she could read herself to sleep. After a few pages of a mystery, drowsiness began to set in. Arabella laid the book down and turned over on her side to face the sketchpad that was propped on her night stand. The light of the moon shown on his beautiful face. Her eyelids became heavier and heavier, slowly she willed herself back to the dream state in which she had encountered her intriguing companion.

****

A strong wind began to blow and a cry of a hawk was carried on the wind. It picked her hip length dark hair up and caused it to whip around her face. She looked around to try and recognize where she was. It was a hill, a place she recognized - a dome actually - Arabella was standing on the top of the pink granite mountain near her home, Enchanted Rock. She had not been there in years, but when she was in high school this had been a favorite place to hike and picnic.

A noise startled her, and just as she started to turn, warm hands slid around her waist from the back. They slipped underneath the silk nightie and moved over her breasts, cupping them gently. Recognition flooded her body as did a total welcoming. Still holding her securely, he eased her back against himself. His hands began a slow dance over her swollen, sensitive breasts. Her nipples hardened and became diamond points of sensitivity. His fingers circled, massaged, lifted and teased the grateful mounds of flesh. Weakness flooded her lower regions and she felt as if it was only his hands on her body that was serving to tether her to the earth. She raised her arms over her head and found his face. She moved her fingers over his features as if memorizing them by touch. She tried to shift in his arms so that they were face to face, but he kept her anchored where she was. He continued to make love to her breasts with his hands, a steady circling, rubbing rhythm that ended every few moments at the end of her nipples, slowly distending them before beginning the sensual ritual all over again.

Her world condensed, until the manipulation of her breasts and nipples was the focus of the universe. An intense heat began building and adding to her torment, his lips and tongue began kissing the curve of her throat and shoulders. A tightening began in her vagina and even though there was no contact made, it began to dew in anticipation of delight. Never before had she known so much joy could be gained from touch alone. When the shivers began, his hands finally moved lower and slid beneath the silken panties to find the hot waiting folds that vibrated ecstatically to his lightest touch. Her hips jerked uncontrollably as she rode his hand, tiny mewls of passion escaping from her lips.

Flushed with release, Arabella relaxed completely into his big, hard body. With a slight pressure, he turned her around and captured her lips with his. As she touched his waist, attempting to gain access to his manhood, his hands grasped hers intertwining their fingers. "Not enough time," he whispered. A vacuum of pressure seemed to pull him backward, "Find me." These final words were spoken as the wind picked up once more and the night enclosed them in nothingness.

****

When day broke Arabella found dampness on her pillow. She had cried during the night, after he had gone. The worst part was that she did not have a great deal more information now than she did yesterday. Guilt tormented her, if she could have just kept her head about her and talked to him. His touch was so intoxicating that her sensual side had completely dominated their encounter. The only clue that she could remember was the location - Enchanted Rock. What that meant she did not know.

Despite the disappointment in her failure to garner his name or anything else about him, she felt absolutely wonderful. Her reaction to this man was beyond anything she had ever thought she was capable of feeling. At his slightest touch, she was primed for passion. Arabella could not comprehend what an actual physical encounter with him would be like, but she had hopes of one day finding out.

She went through her morning regime on automatic, considering what step to take next. Was she meant to find him? Was all of this just a precursor to a future meeting? Did he have any knowledge of her or were they just destined to meet in their dreams?

****

After Evangeline had arrived at Nanette's elegant old home on Constance Street in the Lower Garden District of New Orleans, carefully controlled chaos had been the order of the day. Angelique had insisted that time be taken to adequately pack everything that she thought would be needed for the trip. Nanette had allowed Angelique to have her way, but the older woman had done her part to pack items that she felt the younger two would overlook. She gathered her spell books, plenty of broken glass, nails, a case of canning jars and a five gallon bucket of red brick dust. These things would be necessary for the protection ritual she intended to perform upon her arrival.

Not knowing how long they would be gone, there was no question that the cats had to be readied for the trip. The two large, black cats had been brought to their house one night by a young boy who could not bear for them to be taken to the pound. His parents would not allow him to keep them and he knew that the Beauregaurde house would be a safe haven for the felines. Both of the cats were boys and Evangeline had named them in honor of two rappers that she liked to listen to, 'Two-Bits' and 'Slim Pickins'. Although Bits was heavier than Pickins', Pickins' was certainly not slim. While they were beloved, the cats could not be classified as familiars. However, when a spell or ritual was being carried out the cats were usually close by, so who was to say whether they lent power to the workings or not.

The black Jaguar sedan had been loaded quickly and they gassed up on the way out of New Orleans. Angelique had driven out of the Crescent City about midnight and had headed west on Interstate 10. She had not stayed on the interstate, but cut up north through the middle of the state and crossed the Sabine River as the sun was coming up.

Evangeline took over the driving for the last five hours as they headed through the pine forests of East Texas. Nanette had dozed for several hours and Evangeline had rested for a little while, but Angelique remained alert. Her eyes constantly watched everything they passed. Angelique saw things that no one else saw.

Angelique had a gift. She knew all gifts had their reasons, but this gift was a great burden to bear. Angelique could see and speak to the spirits of the dead - and the dead were everywhere. New Orleans was awash in the dead. The Katrina dead were the most active in New Orleans at the present. Mercifully, Alcee and Aimee had never made an appearance. The Katrina dead who had lingered behind were angry for what had happened to them and what had happened to their city.

Even in the home on Constance Avenue, the dead walked besides the living. Nanette's mother, Patrice, still resided with the family – even though she had died thirty years previously. Evangeline and Nanette were usually unaware of her presence unless she insisted Angelique pass a message to her daughter or her granddaughter.

Angelique did not pretend to understand all there was to know about being dead, but she did know that the choice to haunt or go beyond the veil did not seem to always be theirs to make. Moving on or going to the light did not seem to be an option for everyone. Some souls seemed to be chained to a location as if by an unseen rope. Despite her exposure to Catholic doctrine, Angelique suspected that reincarnation was what waited for a soul once they let go of their earthly bonds, but Angelique had seen some souls that had been ghosts for hundreds of years. She supposed there were just some things one did not find out until you were a ghost yourself.

Driving down the road, even in the black dark, Angelique could still see ghosts. Despite the cliché, it was true, they glowed - - they gave off their own ethereal light. Sometimes they moved as orbs or balls of light, when they were in that form Angelique did not notice them as much. Modern day ghost hunters had discovered the orb phenomenon in digital photographs, but Angelique could see with her natural eyes what even the cameras at times could not. While driving down the road from New Orleans, their car had passed ghosts standing on the side of the highway at scenes of tragic car accidents that had taken their life years ago. They passed homes where Angelique could see the dead standing in the yard or sitting in a porch swing. To Angelique's eyes, cemeteries were especially unnerving after dark, because she could see the glowing forms of the residents walking among the graves. During the day, it was different – the glow of the dead was not as evident and they looked like anyone else from a distance, unless the clothing or the oddity of their movements betrayed their status.

Evangeline drove steadily, stopping only for coffee and a bathroom break in Lufkin, a small town in East Texas. It was during this break that Nanette called Arabella to let her know that they were on their way. After talking to her granddaughter, Nanette shook with nervousness; she could not let death steal another member of her family.

As they resumed their journey, Nanette continued to feel trepidations. After only going a few miles, she visibly shook. "My, I don't like this portion of the road. It doesn't feel right."

Angelique looked on either side of the narrow highway. It was lined with thick, pine forest on both the right and the left. "Something bad happened here."

This intrigued Evangeline, she did not normally question Angelique about her gift or what she could see. Most of the time she just wanted to see the world through clear eyes, unburdened by the reality of spirits and specters. "What do you see Angelique?"

"I see pioneers or settlers; I see covered wagons and horses – but something has gone terribly wrong. They are bloody and torn; it was a massacre. They were beset upon by Indians. They keep pointing as if to show the way." Angelique spoke softly and evenly without displaying any emotion whatsoever. These things bothered her much more than she ever let on.

Nanette had been sitting there quietly, but she could sense them also. "They think they are protecting people. They are warning them of a danger that does not even exist anymore."

Evangeline shivered a bit; glad that her gift was not the same as that of her grandmother and Angelique. Her gift was truly unique. She could read the living, as she had in the magick shop – but that gift was rather common. The truly great gift that Evangeline possessed was one regarding the weather; she could make it rain or she could stop the rain. She could raise a storm and call down lightning. Perhaps she could even make snow – she did not know, she had never tried. Maybe, this Yule she would give calling the snow a whirl, that is, if it didn't snow in Austin on its own. She admitted that it was always a greater possibility of snow in the Texas hill country than it was in costal New Orleans. Evangeline had inherited this gift from her great grandmother Patrice who had used it to great benefit on the Louisiana farm where she had lived.

They were getting close, going through Austin on Interstate 35; they passed the University of Texas on the right as they were heading south toward San Antonio. She could see the Tower and the Daryl K. Royal Memorial Stadium where the Longhorns played their awesome game of football. If Nanette were not so tense about what she saw while scrying, Evangeline would have brought up her desire to transfer to UT again. Maybe after all of this had worked it out she could present her case again.

The miles were passing quickly; soon they would be at the exit that would take them to *Wildflower Way*.

****

The call that Arabella had received from her grandmother had not come as a complete surprise. She was glad to welcome her family to *Wildflower Way* for an extended stay; this big house could be a lonely place at times. The only thing that bothered her was that between her grandmother's concern after her scrying session and the turmoil over poor Kathy and Lea's disappearance, there was very little time left to concentrate on *him*. Memories of the midnight interlude that they had shared the night before were hot enough to cause her to break out into a proverbial sweat.

She was tempted to drop everything and head out to E-Rock to see if she could pick up anything from just being at the scene of their encounter. Right now, however, she just had too many irons in the fire – but that idea was high on her list. Maybe she could get Evangeline to go out with her later today or tomorrow.

Arabella had freshened and prepped all four guest rooms after she had talked to Nanette. She had put Angelique in the pale yellow bedroom that she preferred and Nanette in the room that overlooked the creek. Her grandmother preferred a room with a window that faced the west; she had always hated the morning rays of the sun to intrude upon her morning slumber. It had often crossed Arabella's mind that her grandmother was part vampire since she was so much more of a night owl than the rest of the family, and absolutely abhorred the bright rays of the sun. Nanette always said that it was because her eyes were weak, but Arabella liked to kid her about it anyway.

One of Nanette's great, great grandmothers had come to New Orleans from France as one of the infamous 'casket girls', young women brought across the sea as prospective brides for well-to-do Creole gentlemen. This had been in the early 1700's and the term 'casket girls' had come from the oblong cases filled with their trousseaus that had been furnished the girls by either the French government or their families, if they had been able. For the most part the young women had been from orphanages, as had Nanette's ancestor, Genevieve. The greatest gift that Genevieve had brought with her had been ancient, magical knowledge that had been passed down to her from those that had walked the path of the moon and had lit bright bon fires in the name of the Great Mother, the queen of heaven. After Genevieve's assimilation into the unique melting pot that was South Louisiana, she allowed her European pagan ways to meld with what she learned from her house slaves who had been both Haitian black and American Cherokee. Genevieve had been one of the first to practice the magical mix that came from uniting three diverse cultures into one mystical gumbo that was now called hoodoo.

Arabella waited until she knew her mother was probably up before giving her a ring. She wanted to call and tell her that Nanette and the others were on their way and that she was welcome to head on north if she was free to do so. After only two rings her mother answered.

"Hello darling – how did you sleep?" Her mother's voice literally purred the provocative question. Well, Arabella didn't have to wonder if Elizabeth had picked up on her daughter's x-rated dreams.

"Mother . . . "Arabella pronounced the personal pronoun with mostly mock warning. "Please . . . "she felt like she was fourteen years old again.

"I'm not judging, dear." Elizabeth laughed. "Actually, I'm jealous. I wish my nights were filled with such amorous adventure. Who is he, by the way? I don't know him, or do I?"

"Mother, he isn't . . . I mean . . . there isn't, oh shoot. I don't know what I mean. I'll explain it to you the best I can when you get here."

"Actually, I'm almost out the door. Mother and the rest are on their way aren't they?"

"Can't hide anything from you, can we?"

"Never could." there was a pause as if she was checking her watch. "I'll be there in about five hours.'

"Take care." Arabella murmured, "See you soon." She blew out a long breath; all of a sudden her life was becoming quite complicated.

☾* ~ Chapter III ~ *☽

He could hear the gentle buzz of the overhead fluorescent lights. Jade lay perfectly still. After all, he couldn't move a muscle. He wasn't getting any better and evidently he never would. Even though Dr. Reynolds and the others were not convinced he had heard or understood, they had gently told him that he was a tetraplegic. Jade knew about being a paraplegic or a quadriplegic, but apparently tetraplegic was a whole different ball game. Life was now a burden – a horror – and he did not even have the personal power or ability to bring his nightmare to an end.

A nurse had come in and read a legal document to him. She was probably required to do so just in case there was a chance that he could understand. She told him he was being transferred to a long term care facility called ***Tranquility Place***. Jade would have gagged if he could at the sappy name – he knew there would be no tranquility for him. Every moment was sheer hell, machines were keeping him alive and his care takers were not even thoughtful enough to turn on a TV on the slim chance that he would be aware of it. So all he had to look at was the ceiling, he was not even propped up enough to see around his own room. With no close family of his own, and a fiancé who had been cold enough to have left her engagement ring lying on his chest; Jade only had Reese to check on him and even his visits were getting fewer and farther apart. He was beginning to believe what the doctors said. The mercurial rise in the world of politics was not going to happen for the new darling of the Austin political scene.

The nurse had said he would be transferred to ***Tranquility Place*** in the morning. Sleep was still his greatest comfort; he would have slept all of the time if he had a choice. In his dreams last night, Jade had met the dark haired beauty once again. The excitement and pleasure he had felt with her had put to shame he pallid, one-sided sex that he had experienced with Kate. Kate had just lain there like a limp doll; seemingly unaffected by any feelings whatsoever. He had been captivated by her cool beauty and she had wanted him for his reputation. She was envied by other members of the country club set for her conquest of the rich, eligible bachelor who appeared to have such a bright future.

Now he guessed he was still rich, but it would be a stretch to call him eligible, and he would certainly never be governor of Texas.

For ninety percent of the time, when he was awake – he was alone – and the loneliness was awful, but when he could sleep – he had the most incredible dreams. He pictured her in his mind's eye. She was tall, but not nearly as tall as he was. Her skin was creamy and golden, her hair a silky, black waterfall that hung straight to her hips. Gentle brown eyes that shone like stars and a body that was the sweetest, most luscious package he had ever seen. Her breasts were full, round and incredibly sensitive. Her waist was small, her hips rounded and sexy – and those incredible long legs that wrapped around his hips perfectly. He longed to be with her again.

Never before in his life had he dreamed what seemed to be a continued scenario – same person, same place and same incredible circumstances. What if he couldn't get back to her? What if he never dreamed of her again? He would go stark raving mad; maybe he already was. Last night, he had actually pled with the woman in his dreams to find him, to come to him. Incredible as it seemed – on some level the woman was real to him, more real to him than this hospital bed or the tubes that were keeping the breath flowing to his lungs. When they touched, he could feel her skin, warm and smooth. When they kissed, he could feel her breath, sweet and hot. He prayed that one night he could find a way to stay in her world and be the man she thought that he was. He closed his eyes and willed himself to be at her side.

****

Arabella knew that Rachel would call again and she did. How could she blame her? She would do the exact same thing Rachel was doing, and that was grasping at any and every straw that she could find. Before leaving, Arabella checked the time. It was just after ten in the morning, so there was time for her to go the Townsend place before Evangeline and the others arrived.

Arabella climbed into her Jag convertible and drove the slight distance that separated their homes. Only one neighbor lived between them and it was one Arabella avoided like the plague. Lyle Sessions was a man to be avoided. He had nothing to do with Arabella and she had nothing to do with him. She refused to have any outside cats because if they just happened to wander onto his property he would kill them. Although he would never admit it to her face, he had bragged to another neighbor that he had shot her Siamese cat, Carter. Not ever wanting to risk that again, Arabella kept her animals indoors and carted a sandbox back and forth every day. If it had not been for the old bricklayer, Lyle Sessions, she could have walked from her house to Rachel's in a matter of minutes. Crossing Sessions land was forbidden for Arabella or her family. Mr. Sessions was a born-again Christian, or so he said, but Arabella seriously doubted that even God would have anything to do with that piece of human refuse. If this were colonial times, Mr. Sessions would have been ready to burn or stone Arabella.

Several cars, including a police cruiser, sat in the driveway of the Townsend home. Arabella would rather have not had an audience for what she was about to do. She had tried to tell Rachel that it would be wise to wait until her Mother and grandmother arrived. Whatever power that Arabella had was magnified and multiplied in Nanette and Elizabeth. Rachel wanted someone to do something right then and Arabella did not have the heart to say no, so she went on over to see what she could do.

When she exited her vehicle, she saw Rachel sitting on her patio with two men. She did not recognize either of them but the younger guy wore a uniform and the other was a ruggedly handsome man in a trench coat. A twinge of knowledge or insight crept into her mind and she knew that the older man was a homicide detective. As she approached the group she could not help but overhear the conversation. "I understand, Mrs. Townsend, but there is absolutely no evidence that anything has happened to your daughter and granddaughter. We have put out an alert and sent out pictures to all area stations and we have calls going out checking all hospitals and, uh, morgues to see if there is anyone out there that might have seen your family."

Rachel lowered her face into her hands and wept. Arabella moved up closer and just stood there waiting for an opportune moment to offer her services. Rachel would probably want to get rid of these men before letting Arabella walk the scene. Arabella was quite sure that Rachel would not want it advertised that she had engaged the help of a witch. She had worn her large quartz crystal necklace and her black onyx ring, items that would increase her awareness. To her surprise, Rachel announced her in a way that she had not anticipated. "Oh, Arabella thank God you're here. Officer Myers, Detective Garrison this is my neighbor, Arabella Landry. She has a gift and I have seen her use it. I've asked her to come over and see if she can tell us anything more than we already know." Rachel actually got up and embraced Arabella. It was amazing how a person could change when faced with a devastating loss.

"Are you a psychic?" Officer Myers asked with an audible sneer in his voice.

"No, not exactly." Arabella would not willingly explain her lifestyle to someone who dripped disdain with every word. Rachel had the good grace to look remorseful; after all, it had been she who had judged Arabella harshly in the past.

"Well, I don't see. . ." Myers began to speak but Detective Garrison held up a hand and stopped him. It was obvious that Garrison was Myers's superior. "Let's leave these ladies to visit. Rachel, I'll get back with you just as soon as I have anything to tell you. Stay by the phone, it wouldn't surprise me a bit if you didn't receive a call from that daughter of yours just any time."

A sob tore through Rachel's throat and Arabella knew that Rachel prayed the detective was right. They stood and watched the men get into their separate cars and leave. Rachel then took Arabella by the arm and led her into the house. It had been years since Arabella had been in the home, but as she entered, memories came flooding back. They were memories of more innocent times when the future was anything they chose to make it. Arabella felt good about her life, and if she could help Kathy she would.

"Walk around, Arabella, and see if you sense anything." Rachel watched her with hope-hungry eyes. Arabella did as she was asked. She walked through the kitchen, running her hands over the granite countertops. A child's small cereal bowl sat on the counter and Arabella picked it up and held it gently. She laid it down and walked over to the kitchen window that looked out into the back yard that bordered the woods between their homes. As she looked out the window, her vision blurred as if for a moment she was looking through eyes that were not her own. She reached up and grasped the crystal and brought it to the center of her forehead. The colors in her mind muted and she could hear a voice, an angry voice screaming. 'You whoring bitch!' Arabella jumped as if someone had hit her.

She turned to look at Rachel. "Someone came into the house; Kathy let a man in the house."

"Who?" Rachel demanded.

"I can't see him, but Kathy made it possible for him to enter your home." Arabella walked out the back door and into the grassy yard. How she wished that the yard was dirt and not carefully manicured grass so thick and green that it was like the deepest, most luxurious carpet. There was no way that any footprint could be detected. As she moved about the yard she began to sense something else. She could feel Kathy, the panic and fear that were coursing through her body, but more than that she could feel the fierce protectiveness that the young woman felt for her

child. "I can't give you details, but they did come outside."
"So, do you feel that they were forced to leave with this man?"
"I get that impression, Rachel." Arabella wanted to tell the anxious woman more, but she wasn't confident in her ability to interpret what she was seeing. "It is only a matter of hours and my family will be here and I am positive that they can help you. I promise that I will bring them over just as soon as they get here."
"All right. I don't guess I have much choice. The police, they think that Kathy and Lea have left with someone voluntarily. You see Kathy allowing a man to come into my home and then you see them leaving. You also feel that the man was violent, that he attacked my girls. Why can't the police find any evidence of this? Why won't they go and look for Kathy and Lea?"
"Maybe they don't have any substantial leads. I hate to keep repeating myself, but when mother and grandmother get here they'll be able to tell you more than I have. Please believe me, they will help."

****

Arabella left the distraught woman and returned to *Wildflower Way*. She was not surprised to see her grandmother's car already sitting in the driveway. The doors had not been locked, so she knew that she would find them already making themselves at home. Despite the serious circumstances, she was excited at the prospect to see them. She literally ran up the walk and bounded up the steps. "I'm home! Where are you guys?"
"In here!" Evangeline answered. The two cousins hugged with glee and Nanette and Angelique were there to embrace Arabella as soon as Evangeline turned her loose.
"I am so glad you are here. Mother is on her way. I talked to her a few hours ago."
"Let me look at you," Nanette took her hand and twirled her around. "You look beautiful, cher." Nanette saw an Arabella that the mirror did not reveal. Arabella did not realize how truly beautiful she was. She was slightly taller than Evangeline who was about five-seven. Her hair

was full, straight and hung almost to her hips, its color almost black with hints of burnished copper. Eyes that were a shade of brown, reminiscent of European dark chocolate, were framed by lashes, thick and long. High cheek bones and a graceful mouth were set in an aquiline face granted to her by her French ancestry. "Who is he?" Nanette asked out of the blue.

"What?" Arabella was incredulous. How fortunate she wasn't actually trying to keep the whole thing a secret.

"You look loved." Angelique said quietly.

Evangeline's eyes held a million questions, but she knew Arabella would tell her everything when the right time came.

"I saw love in the cauldron last night." Nanette announced as she headed back to the comfortable chair by the fireplace. "I didn't know if it would be you or your mother. Her energy is still highly associated with this place." Arabella did not know what to say. She knew this had not been the revelation that had sent Nanette across the river into Texas. Her silence did not deter Nanette in the slightest. "Is it you?"

"Not in the conventional sense." Arabella took a deep breath and plunged ahead. There was no use trying to keep anything from this bunch. At that moment, before Arabella could elaborate Elizabeth breezed in.

"Now the festivities can begin." Elizabeth made the rounds properly, greeting each one. "Are you talking about Arabella's lover?"

Her mother had absolutely no manners, Arabella thought.

"I am replete with manners, my dear."

"Mother, stop reading my mind!" She wished that she could get mad at her mother, but she couldn't. Elizabeth was just too cute, by far. Maybe, she would feel better if she just laid bare her soul. "All right, all right. Somebody make some coffee and I will explain everything."

At her suggestion, Angelique headed to the kitchen. They all followed her and gathered around the round table that was the center of the French Country kitchen.

Someone had put on a pot of gumbo. The smells were out of this world. "Did you bring that heavenly concoction with you?" Arabella asked.

Angelique answered. "I had started it yesterday and when Nanette decided that we should come, I packed it up."

"The cats came too, I see" Elizabeth noted the two fat black tom cats lounging on the floor in front of the stove. They weren't alone. Arabella's two cats were there also. Amos and Butterbean were Tabbys. Amos was an orange tabby and Butterbean was brindle. They were as spoiled as the rappers. It didn't take long for the coffee to make.

"Spill it." Elizabeth did not waste words.

"For the past two nights, I have been seeing someone – in my dreams." She looked around from face to face. No one looked shocked; they just waited for more information. "I don't remember ever meeting him before, but yet he is very familiar to me. I don't know who he is. I haven't been able to... find out any information . . . . because when we're together . . . "

"They can't keep their hands off of each other long enough to talk." Elizabeth drawled the completion of her sentence.

"Does it feel like a dream, Arabella?" Angelique asked her seriously.

Arabella knew exactly what she meant. "No, it's more than a dream. I can tell the difference. I'm meeting him at Enchanted Rock – not too far from here."

"I know E-Rock," Elizabeth commented as she stirred the seafood stew. "It's enchanted, just like the name says. That place sits on a ley line and the entire thing is made of crystal quartz. That mountain is magick personified. It is a sacred, powerful place."

"So you think the man is more than just a fantasy, not just someone you literally dreamed up?" Evangeline asked thinking the whole thing sounded incredibly romantic.

"Yes, I do. He has said only two things to me. The first was 'come to me' and the second was 'find me'. I know it sounds absurd, but I just know he is a real person.

How do I find him, Grandmother?" Tears were very close to the surface as Arabella laid her head in Nanette's lap.

"We will find him sweetheart; do not doubt that for a moment." Nanette looked up at Angelique for support and the wise woman nodded her head in affirmation.

"I thought we could go to Enchanted Rock and see if we can sense anything there."

"I'll go with you, Arabella." Evangeline assured her. "Do you want to go now?"

"No, it will have to wait until later. I have made a promise to someone and it must be kept." She knew that these three were probably far ahead of her, but Arabella needed to say it all out loud. "Mother, do you remember Kathy Townsend and the awful slumber party where I made the mistake of showing off a little too much?"

"How could I forget? You cried for days. I thought I was going to have to home school you." Elizabeth placed a loving hand on her daughter's head.

"Rachel, her mother, the same woman who shamed me and called me a heathen, phoned me yesterday and begged me to help her. Kathy and her five year old daughter disappeared almost forty-eight hours ago. I read a few things and went over to the house to see if I could pick up any information and what I got wasn't pretty. I saw Kathy and Lea attacked by a man that she allowed to come into their home. I used a pendulum over a map of the area and I placed it as close to their home as I could and it would not budge. The only direction it pulled toward was down. I don't know what else to do. Rachel is going crazy and the police feel that she just left and took the child with her. Mother, I promised Rachel that you and grandmother would go over and see if there was anything that you could do."

"Of course we will, baby." Nanette rose to get her purse. "Somebody turn off that gumbo. We will eat later." Elizabeth did as her mother said. "Angelique, you come with me. If anything really bad happened, you'll know." Nanette stopped her forward progress, "Wait a minute, what am I thinking – this won't wait." She reached into her purse and took out five, red flannel bags. "The reason that we came early was that I saw danger in the scrying bowl. I saw danger and death. There are several things that I intend to do, but until then, I want each one of you to wear this protection gris-gris. It is full of angelica, garlic, mistletoe and a tiger's eye. I have blessed and prayed over this bag and have asked Chango to protect you. It is sealed with Saint Barbara's symbol, a tiny gold sword. Wear it around your neck. It will keep you safe until we can do more. I must figure out what we are up against and then I will know how to proceed." She gave each one of her loved ones a bag and they did as she asked. "Elizabeth, do you know where the Townsend house is?"

"You can almost spit on it from here."

"You have such a way with words, my dear." Nanette had truly missed her daughter. 'Arabella, you and Evangeline go to that mountain and find that boy. Angelique, Elizabeth let's go see about those children."

❰* ~ Chapter IV ~ *❱

The drive to Enchanted Rock from Wimberley was a scenic one. Evangeline loved everything about the Hill Country. She kept pointing out features that caught her eye; an interesting tree, a meandering stream or a quaint farm house. Arabella enjoyed seeing the familiar scenery through her cousin's more appreciate eyes. "Just wait till you see it in the spring; the wildflowers bloom in profusion. Bluebonnets, Indian Paintbrushes, Purple Cone Flowers and Black-eyed Susans will paint the hills more beautifully than any artist ever could."

"It sounds wonderful." Evangeline looked out of the car window wistfully, and then out of the blue, "I've been asking Nanette to let me transfer to UT."

"Really, what did she say?" Arabella would love to have Evangeline that close.

"She said it would break her heart." With that, Evangeline sighed and Arabella thought the less she said the better until she could talk to Nanette herself.

They rounded one more curve and then Enchanted Rock came into view. E-rock was the second largest granite dome in the world, only Stone Mountain in Georgia was bigger.

Arabella turned into the park gate and they were surprised to find that there was a long line of cars waiting to be processed through the park ranger's check station. Apparently, a car of college students were being delayed because one of them had decided it would be a good idea to take a whiz on one of the rocks that framed the entrance. Their vehicle had been pulled over, and the guilty culprit was getting a stern lecture from one of the older female rangers. With bowed head he endured the dressing down, and then thankfully they were allowed to proceed. After only a few more minutes it was their turn to be given a map and directions for parking. They paid the fee and wound around the access road until an open parking spot came into view. Evangeline scanned the fact sheet that was on the back of the map and was surprised to read how immense Enchanted Rock actually was; it covered 640 acres and rose 425 feet in the air.

After parking, they headed toward one of the walking trails. Arabella had decided that they should take The Summit Trail to get to the top of the pink granite dome. Leaving their car, she slung a backpack over her shoulder that she had hastily filled with bottled water, granola bars and a few first aid supplies in case one of them took a tumble. They crossed over the small creek using the stepping stones and walked north until they found the signs that pointed the way to the trail.

"The Tonkawa Indians that used to live in the area called this place the 'singing rock'." Arabella explained as they started the trek upward. "Scientists now say that the eerie singing noise is caused by the cooling of the granite after the hot Texas sun sets."

Both of the girls were anxious to get to the top so they carefully passed several families and a few couples who were enjoying each other's company too much to hurry. Arabella realized that she was nervous, but she really didn't understand why. She did have to admit though, this whole situation was more important to her than she realized.

Evangeline smiled, she had forgotten when Arabella was nervous about something she tended to rattle. The higher she climbed, the more she talked. Facts were spouting out of her the way they did from a tour guide. "Another oddity about E-rock is a translucent green glow that emanates from the surface of the stone at dusk on some moonlit nights. The Indians called it ghost fire, but the geologists say that the glow is solar heat radiation emitted from the slightly radioactive granite. Elizabeth has always said that E-Rock is one giant solar battery."

Not that the information wasn't interesting, but Evangeline would rather Arabella talk about the matter at hand. She jumped into the conversation before additional facts flowed from the older girl. "Arabella, tell me what he looks like."

She only hesitated for a moment and then she began to speak. "He's beautiful. His complexion is golden and he is built really well. His hair is long and he has the cutest smile. His eyes and hair are both golden brown and he is tall, at least six four or more. My head rests right under his chin." Evangeline had no trouble hearing the wistful longing in Arabella's voice.

"It would be better if we could perform the ritual as close to the spot where you have been meeting him as possible. Think back, do you remember any distinguishing features that we could look for to determine where your rendezvous took place?"

Arabella threw her cousin a disparaging glance. "I remember we were on the west side, because I could see over the edge and I also could see the last vestiges of the setting sun directly in front of me. There was a large boulder and one of those gnammas pools or doughnut holes, or whatever you call them, close by with water still standing in it."

"Well, then that's what we will look for." The hike took longer than Evangeline expected and when they finally reached the top, both girls realized that they weren't in as good physical shape as they had thought they were.

The view from the top of the dome was incredible. The wind was blowing briskly and Arabella turned and headed to the west side of the massive rock mountain to see if she could locate the familiar spot.

Evangeline was intrigued by everything and everybody. She stopped and talked to several people just to find out where they were from. Surprisingly, the majority of the people were local. The Hill country is one area that is appreciated by its residents. She finally caught up with Arabella who was standing still as if she was listening for something.

"This is the spot, as best as I can remember," Arabella said quietly. She held her arms up and turned around and around slowly. "Close your eyes, Evangeline. Let yourself tune into the essence of this place." Evangeline did as she was told. "Can you feel it? Enchanted Rock is very spiritual. It should be easy to connect with the Goddess here."

Evangeline followed her cousin's example. She wasn't into ritual as much as Arabella was. In New Orleans, if a spell needed to be done – it was done. She decided to take the bull by the horns. "Put yourself into a trance state and see if you can connect with him."

Arabella was more methodical "Let's cast a circle and call upon the Watchtowers of the East to aid in my search." Even though there were others around, she began to walk in a circle. Taking sea salt from her pocket, she drew a circle on the ground with a steady stream of the purifying mineral. "I cast a circle of perfect love and perfect trust. I call upon the God and the Goddess, the mother and father of all life, the creator of heaven and earth to be with us as we perform the task before us this day. Guardians of the East element of Air, hear our plea. Let the winds of knowledge blow our way as we seek an answer to our questions." After completing the circle, she stood next to her cousin and bowed her head.

Again, Arabella began to speak. "Goddess of the moon, God of the sun, Archangels Michael, Gabriel, Raphael and Uriel hear my voice. Aid me in my quest. I ask that you reveal to me your secrets. Share with me your knowledge. I seek to make contact with the man whom I have met in my dreams. Grant me this boon. Whisper your answer on the wind. I call upon you to reveal to me the identity of the one whom I seek." They stood still as the winds whipped around them. Several people had walked nearer to see what they were up to. No one disturbed them or came close enough to be a distraction. They stood still for several minutes and listened. "Open the circle, Evangeline."

She did as her cousin asked, walking around the circle for a final time and saying, "I open this circle; I thank the ones who have heard our voice. Stay if you will, go if you must. Thank you for your assistance. We are the flow and we are the ebb. We are the weaver and we are the web.

Harm to none, our will be done. So mote it be."

Arabella stepped out of the circle and as close to the edge as she could without endangering herself. She stood very still and as she looked out at the vast expanse of the park, hoping against hope that he was somewhere out there – she felt the touch of a hand lightly brush across her cheek. She jumped slightly and opened her eyes, expecting to see her cousin standing near and offering comfort. There was no one there. Evangeline was standing ten or twelve feet from her watching two small children chasing after a roadrunner that was skittering over the pink granite surface. Arabella placed her own hand over the spot where she had felt his touch. A young man with a baseball cap who had been watching her called out, "Hey, don't get too close to the edge! A guy fell and hurt himself real bad a couple of weeks ago." At his admonishment, Arabella stepped back from the steeper, slick portion of the dome.

When she turned to meet Evangeline to start down the trail, she was surprised to find Evangeline with a curious look on her face. "Do you think that was your answer?"

"What do you mean?" Arabella didn't get it.

"That man just said that someone fell off E-Rock a couple of weeks before. Could that be your guy?"

An odd feeling was working its way through Arabella's heart. "Do you think that was my answer?" Was he hurt? Was he dead? She was confused, hopeful and at the same time scared to death.

"I think it's worth checking out."

****

Jade Landale was panicking. The only lifeline he had to hold to was the escape that he had in his dream state. This time his dream had not turned out as before. It was all very strange; when he had first dropped off to sleep he had been dreaming of his best friend in high school, Todd Reynolds. They had been climbing out at Heuco Tanks which was about 32 miles northeast of El Paso. It was a climb that they had made together several times, but this time Todd fell. It had been Jade's fault, and he had watched his friend fall headfirst down Mushroom boulder.

Jade watched in horror as he bounced off the side like a rag doll. Then it had been as if a magnetic force began to draw him, he tried to fight it, but it was too strong. He had been pulled into a tunnel-like vortex and when at last he became aware of his surroundings, he was back on E Rock.

At first he was thrilled; standing on one side, seemingly where he had left her was his lady. She was so beautiful. His loins tightened at the sight of her. He approached her, but this time she did not respond. It was as if she couldn't see him. He went up to her, but her eyes looked right through him. Her lips were moving, but he did not hear any sound at all. Panicked, he tried to make her look at him. He touched her face with his hand. She jumped – at last acknowledging his presence. Her hand came up and she touched her cheek in the same spot that he had.

Then, cruelly, unwanted hands brought him back to unwelcome reality. He awoke to find that several orderlies were working to move him and all of the machines that he was hooked up to from the room that he had been in for three weeks to wherever they were transferring him to.

They were early, he thought. Time didn't mean much to him. He did know that it was still daylight outside. No one offered him any explanation.

He had so many questions and no answers. Had they given up on him? Were they taking him some place where he would get more individualized care? These questions were important to him, but what was more important was why he was not able to make contact with the beautiful woman on E-rock. She had been his salvation; if he lost her then he would have nothing, absolutely nothing.

****

Elizabeth, Nanette and Angelique made their way up to Rachel Townsend's front door. Already, Elizabeth – by far the most sensitive one in the family – was picking up on the violent act that had led to the disappearance of the mother and the daughter. Rachel came to the door after only a second or two. "Oh, thank you for coming. I have been waiting for you."

The trio entered the home and Elizabeth went on back

to the kitchen, not waiting for an invitation. Nanette took Rachel's hand and held it within her own. "Mrs. Townsend, please accept our condolences. We are so sorry to hear about Kathy and Lea."

"We really don't know anything yet." Rachel was pitiful. Her complexion was ashen gray and Nanette could tell that Rachel knew in her heart what she had not been able to say out loud. Rachel knew that Kathy and the little girl were gone, and they would not be returning. Angelique and Nanette stood on each side of the woman and walked with her into the kitchen where Elizabeth was standing at the sink and looking out at the backyard.

"Did the little dog ever show back up? A white poodle, I think you said?"

"No, and frankly I have been so torn up about the girls that I haven't thought much about the dog."

Elizabeth nodded, and then spoke frankly. "He got rid of the dog first."

Rachel gasped.

"Mrs. Townsend, the man who attacked your daughter and granddaughter came into this house intending on doing them harm. The violence was premeditated."

"Who would do such a thing?"

There was no answer to that question at present. Elizabeth continued, "I don't have a name. The man does not think of himself by a name." She stopped and was very still, "He considers himself to be 'The Righteous'."

None of the others saw Angelique looking out the glass patio door. None of them heard her gasp.

"Mrs. Townsend, may I have a recent picture of Kathy and Lea?" Angelique asked in a very low and even tone. Nanette walked over to her companion. She knew that Angelique could see something they could not.

Angelique had answers.

Rachel walked into the adjacent room and came back with a framed photograph. She handed it to Angelique, who took one look at the picture and then laid it down on the cabinet. She opened the door and walked outside. They slowly followed her as the stately woman walked toward the wooded back of the property.

"What is she doing?" Rachel asked Nanette.

"I'm not sure, but I think that we had better get you a chair." Nanette was almost sure that she knew what was coming.

Angelique walked toward the trees. The mown portion of the back yard ended abruptly in a thickly wooded area that was covered in low, dense underbrush.

This is what Angelique saw: standing at the edge of the trees, pale and covered in blood was Kathy McLemore. She was holding on to the hand of her small daughter.

Even after years of experiencing encounters with the dead, Angelique still felt the dread and the uncertainty that she had felt the very first time she had ever seen a ghost.

Angelique's first time had been at an aunt's wedding when she was six years old. The ceremony had been held in the neighborhood church and Angelique had been asked to be a flower girl. She was very excited and took her job very seriously. As she walked up the aisle, scattering rose petals, Angelique noticed a little girl standing up at the front over by the piano. As she drew closer to the wedding party, who were standing in a semi-circle in front of the altar, Angelique drew a startled, audible breath. She was close enough now to recognize the other girl. It was her cousin, Bettina. The job of flower girl had first been promised to Bettina and now she had arrived to watch someone else do what she had so looked forward to doing herself. Angelique was even wearing the dress that had been sewn originally for Bettina. Angelique began to shake. Her steps slowed down to a crawl. Everyone was watching Angelique as she so carefully stared at the area off to the right near the musical instrument.

Bettina was not happy. The look on the little girl's face sent cold chills down Angelique's back. The wedding party was all looking at Angelique and wondering why she had stopped throwing rose petals halfway down the aisle.

All of this would have been easily solved – the bride would have been glad to include Bettina in the procession – Bettina's mother would have been overjoyed to know that

Bettina had felt like coming to the church – Angelique used to love to play with her favorite cousin . . .

. . . but Bettina had died six weeks earlier from bacterial meningitis.

Angelique looked around the church with horror, but no one else was looking at Bettina. They were all looking at her. No one was aware of Bettina's presence except Angelique. She pulled herself together and took her place at the front of the church. The wedding went on as planned. No one else saw the small, dead girl as she walked up and down the aisle. She stopped at her mother's pew and then her grandmother's. She came and stood by the bride and tried to pinch Angelique's arm. It was all Angelique could do to keep from running from the church screaming. Finally, Bettina left. She walked into the wall on the right side of the church and Angelique never saw her again.

She told her grandmother about it when she got home. Granny Thibodeaux had not been able to go to the wedding; her arthritis would not permit her to leave her home. She had sat Angelique down and explained to her about the gift. It was a gift that they shared; Granny Thibodeaux said that it skipped a generation. Granny's daughter, Angelique's mother could not see spirits but she and Angelique could.

Now today, she was seeing the spirits of Rachel Townsend's family. Angelique came as close to them as they would allow. She attempted to talk to them, but at this time they had no words. They turned slowly and walked to the woods as if they wanted to be followed. Angelique did the only thing she could do, she followed them.

The two ghosts appeared very lifelike. It was obvious that they had been severely beaten around the head and shoulders. They did not look back to see if Angelique was following them, they just continued on their solemn journey. Soon, they came to the remnants of an old well. The concrete curb was still visible that enclosed the top of the well. Vines clung to the sides of the curb and an old piece of rusty tin covered the opening. Kathy and Lea stopped at the well and turned to face Angelique. She did not have to look into the well to know what lay at the bottom.

Back with Rachel, Nanette and Elizabeth quietly sat, waiting on Angelique to return. When she did, one look at her face told them volumes. "Mrs. Townsend, it is my strong belief that your daughter and granddaughter have met a tragic end." Rachel Townsend crumpled over with the news, and if Elizabeth had not supported her, she would have fallen to the ground.

Angelique continued her sad news. "When the police return, have them search in an abandoned well that sits at the back of your property."

Nanette looked at Elizabeth, "Call someone to come."

Elizabeth went in the house to phone the police. Angelique moved near to Nanette and said softly. "We have a bigger problem than you might think."

Nanette walked over to one side with Angelique, "What do you see?"

"Kathy and Lea aren't the only ones here."

Nanette looked at Angelique with horror.

"What do you mean, Angelique?"

"There are at least five others here, all of them women."

Nanette turned and looked at the woods as if this time she would see more. Of course, she saw nothing.

"As I walked behind Kathy and Lea, they just started coming from out of the woods. They want us to know that they, like Kathy and Lea, are here – waiting."

The gumbo was excellent. It was a dish that only improved from reheating. That was fortunate, because it was almost ten at night before they all were able to return to *Wildflower Way* and finally get some supper. So much had happened they, could barely take it all in.

Over at the Townsend's, Detective Garrison and Officer Meyers had found Kathy and Lea's battered bodies in the old well, exactly as Angelique had said they would. Kathy's keys and purse were found with the bodies. Garrison had not said much, but he was taken aback by the accuracy of the information provided by the women.

Elizabeth had asked the detective to call on them the next day. Somehow, she was going to have to convince the detective to look for more bodies buried in the woods. Secretly, she was looking forward to the visit. The detective was a very handsome man.

She was also concerned about the publicity. There was no way that their involvement was going to escape the notice of the media.

Evangeline and Arabella had reported that they had cast a circle at Enchanted Rock and felt that they had made contact. Arabella also told what the young man had said about the accident that had happened there only days earlier. "I assume you are going to follow up on that lead?" Elizabeth asked.

"Of course." Arabella assured them of the obvious.

"And you are planning on meeting him tonight?" Angelique spoke softly and carefully.

"Yes, I am going to perform the same ritual and use the dream pillow as I did last night."

Angelique reached into the pocket of her dress. "I have something for you." She pulled out a sapphire necklace.

"Oh, Angelique, how beautiful." Arabella held out her hand.

"Wear this tonight. It will help you dream and it aids in what they call today, astral travel. You have to realize that this young man may be unaware that he is leaving his body. He may not know that this is anything more than a dream. You must ask him some questions and find out who he is, and if he is in trouble, where he is."

"I will try."

They were about to call it a night and retire upstairs, but Nanette stopped them. "Arabella, before we go to bed, let's check every window and every door to make sure that this place is safe. The things that we have been preoccupied with today are important, but our well being must take first place. Tomorrow, we will put up a ward around this home to keep out any enemy or any evil. For tonight, wear your red gris-gris bags to bed and I will pray for our safety." They listened carefully to their elder relative and did as she requested. Nanette knew there was danger and she felt that it may very well be connected to the murders in the neighborhood, but she did not have the answers yet.

The day had been a long one. Nanette, Angelique and Evangeline had not had more than a couple of hours sleep the night before and they were exhausted. Arabella made sure that everyone had everything they needed before she went to her own room.

She couldn't wait to see what her dreams would bring. After preparing for bed, she placed the sapphire necklace around her neck with the red flannel bag. She could tell that it was very old. She charged it in her right hand and asked the spirit of the stone to allow her to find out his name. The dream pillow was placed underneath her own pillow and she once again smudged the room with the mugwort and lavender. Not wanting a repeat of last night's restless tossing and turning, she opted to begin reading a book from the outset tonight. It was a book on the great Edgar Cayce. who was called 'the sleeping prophet'. He wrote a great deal on astral projection and even though it was very interesting, 'the sleeping prophet' put her right to sleep.

Almost instantly, she was where she had longed to be all day. Even though it had been dark when she went to bed it was now light on Enchanted Rock. Again, she heard the cry of a hawk. Frantically, she turned around in a circle searching the vast top of the pink granite mount. She was all alone. There was no one or nothing in sight. Her heart lurched with deep disappointment. She fell to her knees and began to weep. Despair flooded her soul. What more could she do? With head in hand, Arabella prayed to the gods for mercy and help.

A shadow fell over her face. Lifting her head she saw the object of her desire, kneeling in front of her. She threw her arms around his neck and wept with joy. He drew her close and cupped the back of her head, "It's all right. I'm here."

Arabella found his lips with hers. The kiss this time was tender and full of reverence. "I didn't think you were coming." She held on to him with all the strength she possessed. The solidness of him was a contradiction that she could not bear to examine very closely. Afraid that she would lose herself in his embrace, she forced her mind to think clearly. "This is real isn't it? Tell me your name."

He took a deep breath and rested his head on her shoulder. "My name is Jade, Jade Landale."

She stroked his hair with her hand. Something was desperately wrong. "Jade, come to me. My name is Arabella and I live at **Wildflower Way** in Wimberley, just a few miles from here."

"I can't."

What did that mean? "Then, I will come to you. Jade, how can I find you?" He turned her loose and stood to his feet. She rose also. Arabella held on to him, afraid that he would vanish at any moment.

"I am at Tranquility." One moment, her fingertips knew the warmth of his skin – the next he was gone and all was black.

☾* ~ Chapter V ~ *☽

His name is Jade.
His name is Jade.
His name is Jade.
The litany played over and over again in her mind. She lay in the bed and stretched luxuriously. The world was looking brighter. He had a name. Jade Landale. But the place, *Tranquility*? A furrow marred her perfect brow – tranquility was a state of mind, not a place. Nevertheless, she had somewhere to start.

A tap on her door interrupted her reverie. "Come in."

Evangeline opened the door and eased in to sit on the bed beside her cousin. "Did you learn anything?"

"His name is Jade Landale."

"Jade. That's an unusual name for a guy, but it's a pretty name. What else?"

Arabella sat up in bed and scooted back until she was leaning on the oak headboard. She tided her hair with her hands and rubbed the sleep from her eyes. "I didn't get much more. When I asked where I could find him, he said something strange. He said he was at tranquility."

"Tranquility, what does that mean?"

"Good question, I don't know if it is a place or an emotion. I hope it doesn't mean he's dead."

"Why don't we use a pendulum and ask some questions?"

Arabella brightened. "That's a good idea. Let me get dressed and we'll Google his name and then use the pendulum if we don't find all the answers on the net."

Evangeline left Arabella to get ready. When she went downstairs, coffee was made and breakfast was well on the way. Elizabeth was making French toast. "Hey, baby. Are you hungry?" Arabella realized that she had really missed her mother.

"Yes, as a matter of fact I am." She poured herself a cup of coffee, and not being able to wait a moment longer, opened up the laptop and entered Jade's name in the search engine. Her heart skipped a beat when there were several hits. Evangeline came in about that time and leaned over her shoulder to see what she had found. "Hey, look at this." She clicked on the first website that came up. "Oh, my God. Now, I know why he seemed familiar. Jade is a State Congressmen. Here is a picture of him rock climbing with a local club. A large picture at the top of an article made her gasp. "Mother, look at this."

Evangeline and Elizabeth both leaned closer as Arabella pointed at the tall good-looking blonde man that was hanging by a rope off the side of a cliff. "Oh, he is handsome." Elizabeth whispered.

Then Arabella moved the screen lower. "Oh, please – no."

The headline read: EXPERIENCED CLIMBER, STATE CONGRESSMEN FALLS AT E-ROCK. She quickly scanned down the article until she reached this line. "It is likely that Congressmen Jade Landale will never recover; doctors report that Landale is completely paralyzed and it is unlikely that he will ever leave the hospital. A promising political career has come to a tragic end." Arabella's heart lurched. Her mother placed a comforting hand on her daughter's shoulder.

Tears were streaming down her face. She remembered what the man had told her at Enchanted Rock yesterday. The reality that he was badly hurt was not a possibility that she had let herself consider. In her dreams he was so vital and strong. "How could this be?"

Nanette and Angelique joined the group and Elizabeth softly explained to them what Arabella had found. "I'm so sorry, baby.' Nanette leaned over and kissed her granddaughter. "Does the article say what hospital he is in?"

Arabella finished reading the write-up, but there was no mention as to where Jade Landale was being treated. "No." She backed out of that site and went back to the list of other web addresses that mentioned his name. "Here's something." She clicked on an article in a San Antonio newspaper.

A gasp escaped her lips. The other article had hit hard enough, but this one took her breath away. A smiling Jade Landale was standing at the side of a beautiful blonde. CONGRESSMAN ANNOUNCES ENGAGEMENT. Arabella slowly shut the computer, stood up and exited the room.

Elizabeth started to follow her daughter up the stairs. "Let her be for a while," Nanette stopped her daughter. "Evangeline, get on that thing and see if you can find anything else out about that boy. Something is not right, here. Elizabeth, can't you pick anything up?"

Taking up the French toast that had reached an appetizing golden brown, Elizabeth fixed her mother a plate. "No, I can't sense him at all. I think it's because he has never been here, nor do we have anything here that has ever been in his presence. I have to have some physical contact with an individual before I can hone in on anything."

Evangeline did not find anything more on the internet that related to his accident. She did find several sites devoted to raising support and money for a possible gubernatorial race in his name. After breakfast, she had every intention of going up and checking on her cousin. Before she could head up the stairs, Nanette stopped her.

"Wait a minute, sweetie. We have a big job to do. As much as I would like to help Arabella find her beau, what I came here for trumps it. I saw danger in the waters and I cannot get it out of my head that what happened to those little girls down the road is tied in with it." Nanette's narrative got their attention.

"I see where you're going with this, Mom." Elizabeth helped herself to a second piece of French toast; her perfect figure was not in keeping with her appetite. "Our involvement will not go unnoticed by the killer."

"Absolutely. His first thought will be that the psychic that found the body will more than likely be able to identify him. We must put up a ward to keep him or anyone that would do us harm from coming on to this property."

Angelique stood up and announced, "I'll begin gathering the supplies, Nanette. Time is of the essence."

"I know this is Christmas Eve and what we'd rather be doing is baking, decorating and making eggnog, but it is imperative that we put a wall of protection around this house." No one argued with her. While Angelique readied all the equipment that they would need, Evangeline hurried up to check on Arabella.

When she came to the closed door of the room, Evangeline could hear Arabella crying. She eased the door open and went in and curled up on the bed next to her heartbroken cousin. "Don't give up. Maybe there's an explanation."

"I'm not giving up, he may need help." Evangeline could barely understand the words spoken into the pillow.

"Sit up, so I can talk to you." All of a sudden, Evangeline felt older than her cousin. Arabella did as she was told. Her beautiful face was tear streaked and swollen.

"You have to remember that he may not even understand what is happening to him. He met you in a dream. Some power has linked the two of you together for a reason."

"I have told myself the same thing, Evangeline. I can't believe he is the type of person that would betray a commitment. If he is engaged, what we have is not real to him. More importantly, I must know what has happened to him." She got off the bed and went to the sink to wash her face.

Evangeline followed her into the bathroom. "Grandmother is about to make witch bottles and put out red brick dust. She seems to think that the killer will come after us when he hears that we helped discover the bodies."

Arabella turned and looked at her cousin. "Wow, this is turning into some holiday isn't it?"

Evangeline smiled with typical teenage bravado, "Yea, kind of exciting isn't it?"

****

Angelique and Elizabeth prepared the witch bottles. They took plain canning jars and filled them with sharp objects, such as nails, straight pens and pieces of a broken glass. Then they added rosemary, cactus spines and rose thorns. Finally they finished off with a mixture of red wine and a few drops, each, of their own blood and urine.

"I used to think this was so gross." Elizabeth said.

"It is a very powerful barrier to evil," the older woman said while attaching twine to the neck of the jar.

Nanette walked in. "Sweetie, we won't be hanging these jars," she explained when noticing what Angelique was doing. "We will bury them. If he were to find one of these jars and destroy it, well that would never do. How many did you fix?"

"Nine." Elizabeth answered. "Will that be enough?"

"Yes, three times three – very powerful. We will space them out all around the perimeter of the property. When you have them ready, I want you two to walk with me as we put out the red brick dust. Bring a shovel and we'll bury these at the same time." Nanette got her cane and they exited the back door to begin the ritual.

Elizabeth got a shovel and the three of them headed to the back boundary of Arabella's land. She owned twelve acres and the back of it was bordered by Cypress Creek. They had to go slow, because Nanette was slow. She instructed them to bury the first bottle and then she began. Angelique handed her a gallon bag of red brick dust. She took out a hand full and started to walk. "Ateh malkuth ve-gevurah, ve-gedulah le-olahm amen. Creator of heaven and earth, God and Goddess, Lord and Lady, Mother and Father of all life. Hear my cry, hear my plea. Protect this land. Protect this house. Protect all of this household. I call upon those whom you have created and given power: Michael, Gabriel, Raphael, and Uriel. I call upon the Watchtowers, the Guardians. I call upon the Watchtowers of the East, element of air. I call upon the Watchtowers of the South, element of Fire. I call upon the Watchtowers of the West, element of Water. I call upon the Watchtowers of the North, element of Earth. Allow no one to come over this boundary that would do harm. Allow no enemy to cross this barrier. Stop the feet of those who would do ill.

Turn back any who would attempt evil against us. My will be done. So mote it be." As she talked, she walked, and repeated the same prayer over and over again. Elizabeth could tell that this was taking a lot out of her mother. She watched as her steps slowed and she became short of breath; still Nanette pressed on.

They walked the entire outer edge of the twelve acres. She and Angelique buried all nine witch bottles and Nanette spread bag after bag of red brick dust. When they were through, they had to help Nanette back to the house. On either side of her, they walked her back until she literally fell into her recliner. "I feel better now," she announced. In a few moments she was asleep.

****

Jade opened his eyes to his new surroundings. The room was much the same as the one at the hospital, except this one was painted a pale shade of lavender. There was still the monotonous buzzing of the overhead lighting and the continual hum of the machines that he was hooked up to. His life was so small and boxed up. This time, however, someone had been nice enough to turn on a TV. It was suspended from the ceiling and Bob Barker was proclaiming that 'The Price Was Right'. Soon, he saw his own face come on the screen. The news reporter might as well be reading his eulogy. He listened at them list his accomplishments and he listened at them talk about what could have been. He saw his Chief of Staff, Reese Philips; comment that there was no more to be done and that a special election would have to be called to select someone to fill the rest of his term. Jade watched his friend wipe away tears and turn his back on the camera and walk away.

He was so thirsty. His mouth felt like the Sahara desert. He longed for an ice chip or a sip of cool water. Fat chance of that, since he couldn't swallow. 'God, why didn't you just let me die?' he screamed silently. But wait, something had happened, something pleasant had happened. Then he remembered, it was in his dream. He had told the girl his name and where he was. She had told him that her name was Arabella. 'Arabella', he thought to himself, 'what a beautiful name'. Her name, however, was not nearly as beautiful as she was. If she was real, would she find him? Did he want her to find him, considering the way that he was? The answer was probably . . . no. He would rather she not see him this way. What had possessed him to ask her to find him?

The door to his room opened and two people entered the room. A doctor and a nurse stood at the foot of his bed and gazed down at him. He met their eyes, but they did not attempt to engage him in conversation. "He's all alone, huh? No relatives, no girl friend, only the people who worked for him?"

The nurse glanced at a clipboard in her hand. "His chart said Reese Phillips should be contacted if his condition worsens, that's all. I understand that Mr. Lansdale's fiancé left her ring on the bed and has not returned, either. Mr. Phillips asked that we not let that particular bit of information get out. There's not much chance of that, the public is fickle and the press has stopped calling."

"Pity." The doctor came over to him and shone a light in his eyes. Reflex made him blink. "So nobody's home."

Jade wanted to scream that he could understand every word that the bastards were saying. The next words that came out of the doctor's mouth sent cold chills down his paralyzed spine. "We will give it some time, but if his name drops off the radar and a number of weeks goes by and nobody comes to check on him – this one may be dispensable. After all, who would question his death? Who would begrudge this guy just letting go? He's young, he's strong – every organ is in great shape, it's just his brain can't communicate with his body. Give our contact a call and tell them that in a couple of weeks or so we may have some merchandise for him."

With that horrific announcement the pair left the room.

Suddenly faced with the likelihood of his own demise, Jade Landale wanted to live.

****

After putting out the red brick dust and the witch

bottles, Nanette took a nap. The rest of the clan began preparing for Christmas and Yule festivities. Elizabeth baked cookies and made a chocolate fudge cake. Angelique made chicken and dressing and a sweet potato casserole. Arabella and Evangeline put up a tree and nestled dozens of brightly wrapped presents underneath it.

    Every time Arabella thought about Jade, she trembled. During a break, she had got back on the computer and looked at the engagement picture one more time. If it weren't Christmas Eve, she would have called the girl - a Kate Thompson. Her parents' names were in the engagement announcement and Arabella had gone so far as to track down a telephone number for them. She was tempted to call on the pretense that she was a friend of Jade's and wanted to know his condition after the fall. All in all, this might be the next best step that she could think of. She had tried to call Jade's former office, but either it was closed for the holidays or had been permanently shut down. Her brain told her just to let well enough alone, but her heart demanded that she see this thing through. She promised herself that she would do just that as soon as the holidays were behind them – if she could wait that long.

    ****

    Most of the food they were preparing was for Christmas Day dinner, but Angelique prepared a Seafood Jambalaya for their supper. Along with crusty French bread and a rum raisin bread pudding, the meal was complete. Heavenly smells were wafting through the French Country kitchen when a knock sounded at the front door. Elizabeth went to answer it, with a knowing smile of recognition on her face.

    "Detective Garrison, please come in," she invited with a sultry warm hint in her voice. The man stepped warily through the door as if he were expecting to be ambushed. Elizabeth hid a smile as she appreciated his tall, sexy body and wavy, thick, brown hair.

    "Come into my parlor, said the spider to the fly." Elizabeth just couldn't help herself. She tended to over-enjoy everything. Detective Garrison eyed her cautiously and admitted to himself that he found this woman incredibly sexy. If he just wasn't almost afraid of her, everything would be all right.

He followed her into the kitchen and accepted a mug of thick eggnog. The other ladies were all present. His eyes moved from the eye-catching Elizabeth, to the equally attractive younger girls, to the stately Creole lady, to the obvious Matriarch of the clan -- Nanette Beaureguarde. The talk of the town was that these women were a group of witches. The media was hounding him for more information and he knew that soon, these women would have more publicity than they ever bargained for. He couldn't decide how he felt about it all – this witchcraft angle really had thrown him a curve.

"Sit, Mr. Garrison." Nanette commanded. "Tell us what we can do for you?"

He did as he was told. Clearing his throat, he began to speak. "I came for some answers. I need to understand what happened at the Townsend's yesterday. Don't get me wrong, I am grateful for the information – but right now I have no evidence to point me in any direction, but at the five of you." At the look on their faces, he beat a hasty retreat. "Now, I have enough sense to know that none of you are responsible, or at least that is what my gut is telling me – but I need more help. I need something concrete to work with. I want to understand."

None of the rest of them knew what to say, but Elizabeth burst out laughing. This man was just too cute for words. "I am grateful for your superior gut, Detective. My family and I would not appreciate being labeled suspects, not after our willingness to assist you in your investigation."

He sipped his eggnog and tried to assimilate his thoughts. "First of all, tell me again how you knew where the body was."

Arabella spoke up, after all this was her house. She began to lay the ground work. "It started with me, Detective. When Rachel realized that Kathy and Lea were missing, she came to me. You had told her that it was too soon to file a missing person's report and she did not know what else to do. She couldn't stand just sitting around and doing nothing and she remembered that my family has, uh, powers."

Detective Garrison interrupted Arabella. "Powers, you say. Do you know that people in Wimberley say that you are witches?"

"I am familiar with that description, yes." Arabella admitted. "It does not offend us, Detective Garrison. Most people have an erroneous definition of the word witch, but in our case it is an accurate description."

They watched in amusement as the color drained from his face. Elizabeth took up the explanation, "Don't faint, detective. We won't stick you in the oven and Hansel you. We are not your HBO kind of scary, baby killing witches. We are the kinder, gentler, garden-variety, hedge-witch type."

"There are types?" He found his voice.

Nanette decided to put him out of his misery. "Its okay, Detective. We are not devil worshiping Satanists. Nor are we Wiccan. We are a family that has unique powers that we were born with. Powers that can come to your aid, if you will allow us to assist you."

He sat his cup down and got out his notebook as if he were going to write down what she was telling him. "It's probably best if you don't write all of this down, honey." Nanette cautioned. "People are not very accepting of our abilities. Let us tell you what we know and what we think you should do next. What you do with the information that we give you is entirely up to you." He folded his notebook back up and put in his pocket and waited.

"Arabella here," she pointed to her granddaughter, "has some, what you might call, psychic ability. She can touch items and get mental pictures of the person to whom the item belongs. Sometimes she can get an idea of what the person was doing the last time they held the object, for example."

"That's right," Arabella confirmed. "The day that Rachel Townsend came to see me she brought Kathy's sunglasses and Lea's doll. I touched them and sensed that they had met with foul play. I felt fear and panic and I saw Kathy get hit forcefully by someone – but I could not see her attacker. Then I took a crystal pendulum and I used it to read a map to see if I could determine which way she had been taken." Detective Garrison was watching Arabella intently.

"Go ahead." He urged her.

"The pendulum proved to be frustrating; it was telling me that she did not go anywhere. This turned out to be true, but at the time, I could make no sense of it."

Elizabeth picked up the story next. "My little girl has many other talents, but in the area of psychic ability – she can't hold me a candle to run by. Where she hears whispers, I hear shouts and where she sees snippets of information - I get reels of movie quality cinematic revelations.' She watched the detective's eyes widen. "And yes, I can read your mind, you naughty boy."

The detective had the good grace to blush because he had been thinking what a beautiful mouth this woman had and how he would like to taste to see if it was as good as it looked. He cleared his throat and ignored the comment. "What did you find when you went over to the Townsend's, Elizabeth?" He tested out her first name and liked the way it rolled off of his tongue.

"At Arabella's request, we went over." Elizabeth decided not to muddy the waters by sharing the trouble that Arabella had experienced with Rachel and Kathy years ago. "When we arrived, I began to relive what had happened in the Townsend home. I saw that Kathy had allowed her attacker to enter the back kitchen door. He did not have to break in." At that bit of information, Detective Garrison got his pad back out and wrote that down.

"You're right," he acquiesced. "We did not find any sign of forced entry."

"I don't know if she had the door open because she was calling the dog and he just took that opportunity to force himself in, or if she willingly opened the door for him because she knew him. That information is blocked by the flood of horror and panic when Kathy realized that she and her daughter were in danger. One thing I do know, the attacker killed the little white dog. I definitely picked up that image from his mind. He thought about that dog several times while he was subduing Kathy. The man hates animals."

"What else can you tell me?"

"I saw Kathy try to get Lea to run," Arabella interrupted her mother's story. "I also saw him catch the little girl and then I sensed that he made Kathy carry her out of the yard."

"You can't give me a description of the killer or a name?" The detective asked hopefully.

"No," Elizabeth signed. "It's odd. I get no picture of him at all. It's like he's cloaked. I don't know if that is literally, or figuratively, but no image of him comes through whatsoever. It's really very strange."

"I'm finding the whole thing kind of strange," the detective admitted. "Did you see him kill them?"

Elizabeth looked down at her hands; she had not shared this information with anyone. "I know he hit them with some type of club."

"That's right. They both died from blunt force trauma. We haven't found the murder weapon, yet. Now, tell me how did you know where the bodies were?" He leaned forward with a mix of fascination and excitement.

"That's where I come in, Detective Garrison." His attention turned to the elegant woman of color. "I do not have the same gift that Elizabeth and Arabella have. My gift is not so pleasant." Angelique watched as the detective raised one expressive brow. "I was born with the ability to see those that have passed on. Sometimes they look as real to me as you do; I have been known to mistake them for the living. Other times, it is obvious they are dead. I have encountered transparent beings, people in various stages of death and by that I mean people who look like their body did at the time of death. Kathy and Lea fit into that category. As I stood at the back door of the Townsend home while Elizabeth was getting a feel for the emotions of the place – I saw Kathy and Lea walk from the woods up to the edge of the yard. I saw them as if they were alive, yet horribly beaten and bloody. They had not abandoned the state of their body as it had been in death. I saw their disfigured faces and the dark bruises and Lea's misshapen skull that she received at the hands of her attacker." Angelique spoke so calmly and softly, that it was a sharp contrast to the terrible things that she was describing.

"Did they tell you where their bodies were?" Frankly, the detective could not believe he was asking these questions. Somehow, all of this was ringing true to him. His usually reliable instincts were telling him that these women were speaking what they knew to be fact. He waited for the rely to his question.

"No," Angelique surprisingly said. "Detective, what I am about to tell you is extremely important. I must say it emphatically, and make you understand that as God is my witness what I am about to tell you is the truth."

Tyler Garrison had no idea what to expect. This woman was talking like what she had up said up to this point was easy to swallow. What could be worse? "Go ahead, I'm listening."

"The newly dead can't always find their voice. My experience tells me that their ability to communicate with the living comes with time and experience. There are those who have no desire to interact with this world and they don't attempt to do so. There are others who want to be noticed and who have something to say, and they find ways to make themselves known. Kathy and Lea appeared to me, but they did not speak. What they did do was lead me to their bodies. I followed them back to the abandoned well. They stood by their resting place and waited for me to join them. There's something else I need to tell you also, Detective Garrison."

He waited patiently, not knowing what possibly could come next.

"There are others."

"What others?"

Elizabeth, Arabella, Evangeline and Nanette all watched the exchange with interest. It was obvious that the

Detective was hearing much more than he bargained for.

His apparent incredulity, however, did not deter Angelique from finishing her story.

"Detective Garrison, there are other bodies buried in that same plot of land that is home to the well where you found Kathy and Lea."

"What are you saying, Miss . . . ." then realizing he did not know her last name . . ."Miss Angelique?"

"It's Angelique Fontenot. Detective, what I am saying is that small area of land right behind the Townsend's on Cypress Creek seems to be a killing field. I saw, perhaps, five or six other women walk toward me from out of the wooded area. Not all of them were silent. One young woman with long blonde hair was not afraid to speak to me. She walked up to me, as close as I am to you. She looked as real as you do, also. She said, "You can see us." I replied to her that I could. She said, 'We have been waiting for so long.'

Detective Garrison was entranced, hanging on Angelique's every words. "What else did the ghost say?"

"She said that all of their families deserved to know what had happened to them. They all want to be found, Detective. There are at least half a dozen lost souls waiting to be discovered. I promised that I would bring you to them and that you would find their bodies and let them go home. Maybe you will find evidence of the killer's identity with one of their bodies."

The next words of the Detective were short and sweet.

"Take me to them."

****

As Angelique and Elizabeth readied themselves to go with the Detective, Nanette rose and prepared a plate of food for them to take to the grieving woman. The bodies of Kathy and Lea had not been released to Rachel, mainly because the autopsies had not been completed to the Detective's satisfaction. Much to everyone's disappointment there had been no trace evidence of any kind on the bodies. Whoever had murdered them and dumped their bodies had known exactly what they were doing. The detective realized now that the knowledge the killer had possessed to elude the eagle eye of the forensic team had come with experience. He was just counting on the hope that he had not always been so careful; maybe there would be evidence on one of the earlier bodies – that is, if they found any other bodies. Something told him that the women were not misleading him. He felt like that he could trust them.

Detective Tyler Garrison walked beside Angelique Fontenot and took notes as she walked him through the haunted woods behind the Townsend home. She gave him name after name and they marked spot after spot as the gruesome tale was told.

Elizabeth had not gone on the sad walk with the other pair but had stayed with Rachel Townsend. They were close to the same age and Elizabeth could not help but think back at the sadness that this woman had caused Arabella. She realized, however, the pain inflicted on her daughter was nothing beside the torment that Rachel was going through at the loss of her only child and grandchild. Elizabeth invited her to come and have lunch with them on Christmas Day, but Rachel had said that she was going to her sister's house. While she was issuing that invitation, another one came to her mind. She wondered if the Detective had family, and if he didn't, would he want to spend another day with her? She decided it didn't hurt to ask.

After Angelique and Tyler Garrison had returned to the house, the detective told her that they suspected that there might be more to find on her property, and would it be okay for them to look while she was gone to her sister's. Rachel told the Detective to do whatever he thought best. Elizabeth wanted to leave, but apparently the Detective had a few more questions.

"Mrs. Townsend, I know I asked you this yesterday, but maybe you've had time to think on things a little more. Can you think of anyone who would have wanted to harm Kathy?"

"I'm sorry, Detective. I don't have a better answer for

you today than I did yesterday. I can't think of anyone who would want to hurt my daughter."

"Have you spoken to Lea's father?"

"Oh, yes. Johnny has been here. As you know, Kathy and Johnny have had a rocky relationship. She took her maiden name back after the divorce, but Johnny never gave up. He loved Kathy and his little girl so much. He is absolutely devastated at the tragedy that has come upon our little family. He said he talked to you and that he told you he would cooperate fully. He is heartbroken; I don't suspect him in the least."

"Well, to tell you the truth, I don't either. His alibi checks out, he was on a business trip and stayed in the room with this other guy, who vouches for his whereabouts the whole time. As you know, we took Kathy's computer and we even checked the hard drive on your computer. We found nothing that would raise any suspicions. Am I missing anything, Mrs. Townsend? Think hard, am I leaving any stone unturned?"

"I can't think of anything. We didn't go many places, just around town and to church."

"Is there anyone in your church that you suspect?"

"Well, good heavens, no."

"That's all the questions that I have now, but if you think of anything, please call me. Right now we have no leads, no suspects, and no explanation at all on who might have murdered your family." She promised to call him if she had any information to share.

After he finished with Rachel, the detective drove the other women home. Elizabeth lingered after the others had gone in. The Detective stood by his car door, also reluctant to drive away from this beautiful woman. "This is truly amazing. I have never met anyone like your family, Elizabeth."

"I like you Detective Garrison." Elizabeth was straightforward.

"I like you too, Elizabeth Landry."

"Would you like to eat Christmas Dinner with a bunch of witches?" She pulled no punches.

"I'd be delighted. What time shall I arrive?"

"Be here at eleven in the morning and enjoy the day with us." He was beginning to suspect that he would, indeed, enjoy the day.

****

Arabella had made a potato salad, baked ten dozen sugar cookies and stuffed a stocking for everyone, including Detective Garrison, once she found out that he would be joining them. She was so torn. Ignoring that it was Christmas Eve, she had finally broken down and phoned the home of Jade's fiancé, but a housekeeper had explained to her that they were all on a ski trip and she did not a have a lot of information on Mr. Landale. The only thing she found out from the housekeeper was that Jade was still alive, but he was very badly injured. She did not know what hospital he was in, or maybe she just wouldn't tell Arabella. One startling revelation had come out, the housekeeper had let it slip and it changed everything – Kate Thompson was no longer engaged to Mr. Landale.

****

Jade was not engaged to another woman! Arabella wanted to shout it from the rooftops! She couldn't wait to tell Evangeline. She soon got the chance, it was getting late and Angelique gathered them all to have some of the fragrant jambalaya and bread. When everyone was seated, she made the announcement. "I called Kate Thompson's house and I found out a couple of things."

"What did you find out?" Evangeline asked between bites of French bread.

"Jade is alive, but badly injured, and Kate Thompson is no longer his fiancée."

"Do you think that woman broke up with him because of his injury?" Angelique asked.

"Yes, I do. And I hate it for him, but I am also happy that he is not involved with anyone else, either." Arabella realized that her feelings were very tender and conflicted. "Tonight, I intend to find out what Tranquility means."

"You will." Nanette assured her. "It's meant to be."

Arabella wished that she felt as confident as her

grandmother did. "Speaking of good looking men, what happened with Detective Garrison?"

"He's coming for dinner tomorrow." Elizabeth happily reported. "As for what happened at Rachel's, Tyler had agreed to begin an extensive excavation the day after tomorrow."

"I will be glad for those poor souls to find some comfort. Now, if we can only find the killer." Angelique looked pointedly at Nanette.

Nanette picked up on her train of thought. "Let's follow last night's routine. Double check the windows and doors and everyone wear their red flannel bags. Tomorrow is Christmas Day, so let's all get a good night sleep."

☾* ~ Chapter VI ~ *☽

Arabella was so tired, that all she did was tuck the dream pillow underneath her own pillow and hold on to it as she fell easily asleep. Exhaustion forced her into a dreamless sleep for a few hours, but soon her heart overrode her tired body.

She became aware of a celestial wind that blew the stars across the sky. Enchanted Rock glowed with a strange light and a hawk cried in the distance. She stared out over the rock and gratefully saw him coming from the farthest side of the dome. Her heart dancing with joy, she ran to meet him. She leapt into his arms and he caught her easily. Their lips met with passion and relief. Kissing him deeply was not enough. She wanted all of him. Tearing her mouth from his, she showered his face and neck with kisses. "It's all true. I found your picture on the internet. Then, I found your engagement announcement and I died. I talked to her housekeeper and she told me the wedding was off and I came back to life."

"I want to make love to you; this may be our last few minutes together." What he said made no sense to her. Their time together was just beginning. It was only a matter of days before she found him. Regardless, she could no more resist him than she could deny her next breath. He eased her lace camisole over her head and then reveled in her beauty. His eyes consumed her delicate shape, admiring the sun kissed color of her skin. He reverently cupped the underside of both breasts and lifted them, tracing the shell pink nipples with his fingers. Her head fell back and her arms came up around his neck. He easily picked her up and carried her to a bed of grass nearby. Laying her on her back, he gazed down at her. "You have made hell bearable for me. Let me love you."

She didn't understand everything that he said, but she knew that she wanted him desperately. She held up her arms and welcomed him. He lay down beside her and caressed her face. His eyes studied her features, as if committing them to memory for eternity. He bent down and began kissing her brow, then playfully kissed down the bridge of her nose before capturing her jealous lips. Their tongues intertwined, tasting the passion that had arisen so quickly. His fingers teased her nipples and soon she was picking her hips up from the ground in the soundless rhythm of life. His hand moved lover and eased the satin panties down her legs and out of the way.

Leaving her lips; his mouth began a tortuous, incredible journey down her throat, over her breasts, past her navel and into the petal-soft folds of her femininity. This indeed was a dream, because nothing could have felt so good. He sweetly kissed every inch of her, his tongue foretelling the wonders to come. Moving upward, he found the pulsating, ultra-sensitive pearl and licked it with the tip of his tongue until the constellations crashed and the sun exploded in the sky.

He did not let her leave him. Ridding himself of his jeans, he covered her with his body. He cradled her until she stopped shaking and her breath returned to near normal. When her eyes met his, for the first time she was shy. No one had ever done the things to her that this man had, even if it was in a dream. Putting aside her reticence, she stared boldly at him and reached her hand down between them and touched the hard, hot erection that was so eager for attention. "Please, inside me, please."

He raised himself up, sat back and gently spread her legs. With one hand he opened the tight depths that were moist and aching to be filled. Never leaving her gaze, he lifted each leg and placed them on either side of his thighs. She trembled in anticipation. "Guide me, Arabella." Realizing what he wanted, she reached out and closed her palm around his thick, engorged penis. It moved in her palm and she was fascinated at the life she held in her hand. Arching her hips, she drew him closer until the head of his member was at the moist heart of her vulva. Ever so gently, he eased himself down into her. The warm, wet haven stretched to accept his entrance.

The interior muscles of her womanhood contracted around his hard, male heat. There was no pain, only pleasure. His driving need thrust into her again and again and she felt her desire change from joyful acceptance to a burning hunger. As he maintained the pumping strokes, her legs involuntarily wrapped around his waist and she pushed herself even deeper up onto his rock-hard shaft. She watched his face as the emotions of overwhelming sensation flowed over him. She had never known how insatiable she could be, as she moved to meet him – lifting her hips to rock against him; hot, wet and with voluptuous abandon.

She did not want it to end; she relished every moment and every sensation. Soon, however an urgency began to build and her hands clutched his arms as her entire world condensed down into the pounding strokes that built and built until she could not hold it back one more moment – she climaxed rapturously in pulsating waves of ecstasy.

The ripples of bliss kept her hips rocking as Jade neared his peak. He adjusted her hips so that he could raise himself up and sit upright while he continued to pump into her ultra-sensitive core. Even though he was experiencing paradise with every stroke, he wanted to give her every sensation that he was capable of. With each hand he clasped one of her beautiful full breasts. He knew how sensitive and responsive her nipples were and as he rode her to his pinnacle, he massaged her breasts and teased her nipples. She had not known that she was capable of feeling the euphoria of another climax, but as he increased the speed and the intensity of his movements, she again felt herself building to another earth shattering release. He went with her this time, groaning – his magnificent body shuddering with uninhibited satisfaction.

After every nuance of pleasure had been savored, he reluctantly pulled himself from her and lay down next to her side. He pushed her damp hair back from her face and tenderly kissed the tears from her eyes. "Listen to me Arabella. I have to tell you how happy you have made me.

It's almost over. I heard the doctor say that it was hopeless and they plan to unhook me from the machines and let me die. My organs can be of use to other people and I realize that since there is no hope; I am worth more dead than alive. The only regret I have is leaving you."

She had tried to interrupt him several times, but he had kept two fingers over her lips until he could finish talking. Finally, she reached up and pushed his hands away and cried, "No, no, no – I will come to you. Just tell me how to find you, please don't leave me. I will come to you, immediately. Tell me how to find you!" She pled with him in a voice that broke his heart.

"I know that it is futile, nothing can be done for me. I am selfish, though; I would love to see you. Come to me if you can, I am at a place called Tranquility. Remember, when you come, that it will appear as if I am just a shell. You won't know by looking at me, but I can hear and understand everything that goes on around me." His words tore through her soul. He forced her to look at him, realizing that the winds of reality were about to sweep over them. "Thank you for the most wonderful times of my life. You are unbelievable, a beautiful dream come true."

****

Arabella woke herself up with weeping. Like a child, she wanted to be comforted. Leaving her bed, she sought the consolation of her mother. Walking barefoot down the hall, she gently opened the door of Elizabeth's room and crept in to curl up next to the woman who had always known the right things to say and how to heal every wound.

"What's wrong, baby?" Elizabeth asked as she became conscious of no longer being alone. "Oh, Arabella its Jade isn't it?" She leaned over and turned on the bedside light. "We will find him." As always, when they were together – words, on her part, weren't always necessary. She reached over and gathered her grown daughter into her arms. "Don't cry, sweetie. We will fix this." She glanced over to the digital clock on the bedside table. "It's five-thirty on Christmas morning, the best day in the world for miracles. Go take a shower and get dressed. I will get Mother up and we will get ready, too. After you're dressed, we will look this ***Tranquility*** up on the internet and then we will hightail it out to see about this fella of yours. He may be in the wrong political party, but if you love him – that's all that is important to me."

****

He had missed killing. The rage that made his brain raw seemed to be assuaged to a certain degree. He dreamt of it so often, this taking of life. He knew that this power was his right and his calling. The Lord had told him, in no uncertain terms, that society needed to be cleansed of the impurities that contaminated His creation and he had been sanctified to serve as the Lord's hand of judgment.

He washed his own hands at the sink. Over and over he had washed his hands. The blood was all gone, but the stench of sin remained. He had tried not to touch the bitch and her squalling spawn, but the microscopic germs of their filthiness had seeped through the rubber gloves that he had worn.

There were others that would soon feel the wrath of God. He could read the signs and interpret the scriptures. There was much work to be done. Whores, unbelievers, faggots and ignorant liberals all must be brought to their knees and he had just the rod that was strong enough to beat them into submission.

They thought they were so smart, using the devil to locate the dump where he had thrown the Lord's garbage. Damn pagans! The Bible said that you shouldn't allow a witch to live. He, the Righteous, intended to follow the teachings of Scripture to the letter.

****

On a normal Christmas morning, they would have gotten up and had breakfast. Next, they would have gathered around the tree and opened presents in their pajamas. Today was different. There was important work to be done. Evangeline was helping Arabella search the internet for a place called ***Tranquility***. After only three tries, they hit the jack-pot. *'Tranquility Place'* was an extended care facility. It was located about thirty miles north, near Llano.

Arabella didn't have to wait long. Elizabeth and Nanette got dressed in record time, and Angelique and Evangeline volunteered to stay and get everything ready for Christmas Dinner. Once they found Jade, then a decision would be made as to the wisest way to proceed.

****

They took Nanette's big Jaguar. Elizabeth turned the English car loose and let it run as fast as the law would allow, plus a smidge. Arabella was as nervous as a canary in a cathouse. She knew in her heart that Jade was in terrible danger. She just hoped they would be able to help him when they got there. "Nanette, Jade mentioned that the doctor said there was no hope, that he would not live much longer and his organs would be harvested to give to other people." Nanette could read between the lines and she willed the car to go faster. She wasn't cruel enough to interpret what Arabella had said in its truest terms; those vultures were preparing to kill that boy for spare parts. She began chanting under her breath, a prayer to the gods to break down the barriers and to pave the way for them to come to this boy's aid.

The luxury car ate up the miles and soon they arrived at an isolated, ultra-modern building with manicured lawns and a peaceful fountain out front. There were no gates or guards to maneuver through, so they parked the car and walked through the front door. A half-moon reception desk sat in the middle of a large, tastefully decorated lobby. An older woman sat at the desk, dutifully typing at a computer. "May I help you?"

Arabella stepped forward, "Yes, we're here to see a patient of yours, Mr. Jade Landale."

"One moment please," the receptionist typed in the name and then smiled. "You are Mr. Landale's first visitors. This note says he has no immediate family. I wonder if I should call and check to see if your visit is OK with Mr. Phillips. He is down as Mr. Landale's guardian."

Nanette did not allow Arabella to begin an explanation. She took a deep breath as if inflating her already substantial self. "We don't have time for that. Do you mean to tell me that we are not permitted to see my grandson? On Christmas?" She emphatically asked with clenched jaw.

"You're his grandmother?" The woman appeared flushed and uncertain. "We have no information on a grandmother or any other relative. Oh my, this is highly irregular."

"I would suggest you give us the room number and point the way." Elizabeth advised the shaken woman.

Arabella did not have to say a word. Nanette had her eyes closed and appeared to be praying, although it was highly unlikely that what she was saying could be construed as a prayer. Elizabeth tapped one of her pretty size seven's and after another few moments of semi-panic the woman finally gave in and rose to escort them to Jade's room.

They followed the mouse-like creature that seemed to becoming more mouse-like with every step. She certainly hoped that Nanette hadn't done anything foolish. Much to Arabella's relief, the woman managed to maintain her human form for the duration of the journey. When they reached Private Room No. 17, the woman opened the door and said, "Prepare yourself ladies, Mr. Landale is a tetraplegic. He is completely paralyzed and the extent of his brain function is unknown. His eyes may open, but the Doctor does not believe that he is aware of his surroundings; so he probably won't know you're here." Arabella wanted to scratch the woman's eyes out as she left, but she restrained herself.

Nanette and Elizabeth allowed Arabella to enter the room first. It was dark, a TV was on and machines hummed and beeped their constant readings that validated the fact that they were keeping the body of Jade Landale alive.

She tip-toed into the room and saw him.

It was him, her Jade.

He looked exactly the way she had seen him in her dreams. His eyes were closed and he was paler, his body was as large and powerful as it had been in her dreams, so she knew that he had not been in this condition long enough for his muscles to deteriorate. She walked up to him and placed a hand on his leg. There was no movement. She walked closer and saw his beautiful, golden-blond hair and his precious face. Nanette and Elizabeth were close behind her. Bending over near to him, she touched his face with her finger and whispered his name. "Jade, I'm here."

His eyes flew open and widened slightly. Arabella's heart flipped, he knew that she was here. She turned to Nanette. "He knows we're here. He isn't brain-dead." She turned back to him and stroked his head. "I've found you now, and nothing bad is going to happen to you." There was no change in his expression, but his eyes seemed to soften slightly.

Nanette stepped up and placed her hand on Jade's chest. She pressed down with a slight pressure and cocked her head as if listening to a voice only she could hear. "We can heal this boy, Elizabeth."

Arabella couldn't believe her ears. She had not allowed herself to think past the point of finding Jade. What was to happen next was a question she had not been able to answer. Her grandmother did not make offhand claims, if Nanette thought that Jade could be healed; then Arabella believed her.

Arabella turned to Jade and told him, "Grandmother says that you can be healed. I won't try to explain it to you, but have faith. Nanette Beaureguarde, my grandmother, is a powerful woman. It will be a pleasure explaining this to you later, but for now – don't you dare give up, or worry a moment that we will abandon you. I am going to be right here by your side until you can leave this place."

Anyone else would have told Arabella that she had lost her mind, but Elizabeth and Nanette only looked at one another with satisfaction. Before they could begin to make plans, the door opened and a man entered, flanked by the receptionist and a nurse.

"Who are you people? Don't you realize that this is a very sick man and that you have no right . . . ."

The doctor did not get to say another word before

Elizabeth was up in his face. "We are his family." (Or rather, Elizabeth thought they might one day be) "I know who you are and I know what you do. You won't get the chance to shorten the life of this young man. I am good friends with a police detective, and if you give me one ounce of encouragement, he will be on you like white on rice. A criminal investigation would tear up your play house, wouldn't it Doctor?"

The doctor replaced a pen in his pocket, "Congressman or no congressman, you have twenty four hours to find this patient a new place to stay."

"That won't be a problem." Elizabeth growled.

"What are we going to do?" Arabella asked.

"Twenty four hours is more than enough time," Nanette patted her granddaughter on the shoulder. "Now, don't you worry. Your mother and I are going back to the house and gather up what we need. You stay here and we will come back and when we're through – we will all leave together." When she said all – Nanette gestured toward the still body of Jade Landale.

****

Jade was shocked. Arabella had found him – and they said that he could be healed!?! Hope and doubt warred for dominance within his mind. How could they heal him? Did they know a specialist? Did they know a miracle worker? Jade knew he had to wait and see, but Arabella was by his side and he finally felt a ray of hope warm his heart. Besides, it wasn't as if he were going anywhere.

He wished she would move closer so he could see her better. She looked exactly as she had only hours ago when he had made love to her on Enchanted Rock. She glanced at him, and it was as if she were reading his mind; she actually blushed. She came close and kissed him on the forehead. "I hope you remember our dreams and don't just think I am some crazy lady come by to kidnap and molest you."

Of course, he couldn't reply. He looked straight into her eyes and tried to convey trust and faith. He had no idea if she comprehended it at all.

Arabella pulled a chair over next to the bed and sat with her hand over his, waiting.

****

"Let's go out and water some of the plants in the greenhouses." Angelique knew that Arabella had been too busy to take care of every day duties.

"Sure," Evangeline rose to help her. They headed out the back through the sun room. In most of the greenhouses, Arabella had automatic sprinkler systems, but one of the houses held violets and other delicates that grew better if they were carefully watered from the bottom.

Angelique opened the back door and held it open for Evangeline to catch it, as she did one of the Rappers ran out between them, full sprint.

"Slim Pickins, you darn cat, come back here!" Evangeline yelled at the errant cat. He paid absolutely no attention to her, he was tired of being in the house with those two grouchy Texas cats and he needed some air. The faster that Evangeline ran after him, the faster he ran away from her. He was heading full tilt for the woods. Evangeline knew that if she did not keep him in sight, she might lose him.

"Pickins, please stop," she begged the cat. He slowed a bit, but he did not turn around. She lunged at him, but he evaded her quite easily, despite his chubbiness.

Evangeline forged onward, determined to catch her cat. Suddenly, every sense she possessed went on red alert. She stopped in her tracks.

Someone else was in the woods.

"Pickins, stop! I command you to return to the house!" She spoke with every bit of authority that she could muster. The words were sent out with magical force and the cat had no choice but to slow his sprint and circle back the way he came. He didn't look happy about it, but the spirits of the woods were blocking his path.

Evangeline stood very still and very quite. She listened for any tell-tale foot fall, or the sounds of a breath being taken. She heard nothing, but she felt what she could not hear. Danger was immediate. She glanced back and measured the distance to safety. Too far. She had passed over the red brick dust barrier and was no longer on Landry land.

****

He had watched her running toward him. For some reason, he wasn't able to come closer. Every time he tried to move forward, his legs refused. They would begin tingling and burning with great intensity and he would find no relief until he backed up. So, he stayed where he was. For the last two days he had kept a constant vigil of the witches' house. He had wanted to sneak onto the property and see if he could catch one of them off by themselves. That was what the Lord wanted, for him to take one of these heathens and purge her of the wickedness that blackened her soul. Patience had paid off, now he didn't have to go to them – one of the witches was coming to him.

****

"Christmas dinner will just have to be postponed until Christmas supper." Nanette commented as she and Elizabeth drove south from Tranquility Place.

'That will be fine, this is more important."

"Take me to that place that Arabella has been dreaming about."

Elizabeth put on her blinker as they came to a cross roads so she could do as her mother requested. "Enchanted Rock? Why are we going there?"

"I need to find a piece of fossil or petrified wood or bone from there."

"Why do we need that?" Elizabeth was not asking because she didn't want to take the time, she knew her mother had a specific idea in her mind and she wanted to understand. Her mother possessed invaluable knowledge.

"A piece of fossil is necessary for our healing ritual. It's sympathy magic; the fossil was once alive and now it is stiff and lifeless like a paralyzed person."

"Enchanted Rock is a big place, a fossil might be hard to find."

"Well, honey – we'll just have to call it up." With that declaration she let Elizabeth drive in silence. They had to

double back, north, once they hit the right road and before long they could see the granite mountain.
"It's beautiful isn't it?" Elizabeth asked.
"Yes, it is and it's going to be cold, too" Despite it being Christmas morning, there were other people at the park. Elizabeth paid the fee and found a parking place.
"Mother, I don't see how we are going to walk up that trail in these heels. We didn't come dressed for this," Elizabeth grumbled.
"We won't have too. Just help me get a little closer and off this parking lot concrete" Elizabeth held her mother's arm as they edged closer to the pink dome. A cold wind whipped their clothes and almost took their breath away.
"Now what?"
"Patience, child." Nanette stood still and listened to the wind. Finally, she began to speak.
"Come to me fossil, ancient as the earth
I know your power, I know your worth
Earth, air, water, fire
Help me find what I desire
Candle, cup. Wind and seed
Help me find what I need."
Elizabeth watched her mother. "How do you come up with these rhymes so fast?"
Nanette gave her daughter a withering look. "Rhymes add power, they fuel my intent." She began to turn around, looking on the ground. "Your eyes are better than mine, Elizabeth. Walk around and look closely, we should find a fossil very close to where we're standing now."
Elizabeth began a widening circle around her mother, watching the ground for a piece of bone or any rock that would catch her eye. A spiral shape jumped out at her.
Elizabeth leaned over and picked up the small rock. "Look mother, it's an ammonite. I remember reading about these; they were once a type of squid that lived in a shell. They became extinct with the dinosaurs."
She handed it to her mother. Nanette was pleased, "That's exactly what I'm looking for. This is exactly what I need. Look at the shape – it's the horns of Ammon, the

healing spiral, the Golden Ratio. This will add great power to our healing ritual."

"You know, we're not supposed to remove stuff like this from the park. It says so in great big letters on the paper the ranger gave us."

Nanette slipped it in her pocket. "Then we'll bring it back when we're through with it."

☾* ~ Chapter VII ~ *☽

It was obvious to Arabella that she had thwarted the doctor's nefarious plans and he was not happy about it. Three times the doctor had returned to perform some test or another. Arabella was sure that this was the most attention Jade had received since he had been admitted. She only moved from Jade's side long enough for them to perform their perfunctory examinations.

When they were alone, she returned to his side. "Jade, I need to tell you something before my mother and grandmother return." She looked steadily into his eyes, hoping he could understand her. "What we are about to do is unconventional. My family practices magic; I know it sounds farfetched, but it's real. I have grown up with it, so its everyday stuff for me. Don't be nervous, nothing will happen that will make you uncomfortable in any way. I don't know what has drawn us together, but a power greater than us has ordained this and I know that we will be able to help you."

Thoughts of what they had done together in her dreams past through her mind's eye and she felt a flush of heat travel upward to her face. She picked up his hand and looked at it; yes it was familiar to her. She knew his body intimately, as he knew hers. "I have so much to tell you. When you are better, we will make our dreams come true – that is if you still want to.. . . . . ." She wished she could be certain that this was not all one sided. This man might be lying here, wondering 'who in the hell' these nuts were. Arabella shook her head and pushed these thoughts away. Time would tell.

When Nanette and Elizabeth arrived at *Wildflower Way*, they found the house empty. "Angelique, Evangeline!" Nanette called loudly. Elizabeth searched through all the rooms before checking the outside. She found Angelique at the back of the yard putting on a pair of boots.

"She's gone." Angelique stated flatly.

"Evangeline?" Elizabeth suddenly felt nauseous. "How long has she been out there?"

"Just a few minutes, she followed one of the black cats that ran out of the house."

"There comes the cat, but she has other company, the bad kind." Elizabeth was seeing things in her mind's eye that caused her blood to run cold. "I've got to get out of these damn heels; some psychic I am. Wait here, I'll be right back." As she opened the door, the fat, black cat ran through it.

Evangeline tried to keep her wits about her. She knew that she only had mere seconds. The very air was charged with electricity. The woods were so thick here that she knew he could be very close to her and she wouldn't be aware of it. If she turned her back on him and tried to run, he would most likely overtake her. She needed a diversion and she knew it would have to be one she created herself.

She held her hands up to the skies.

"Element of Air hear my cry.

Send a storm, let lightning fly

Winds will blow and rain will fall

Air, Fire, Wind, Water, hear my call.

She had nothing with her to fuel her spell. Normally, she would have poured out rice and water as an offering to the gods. Instead, she began quoting a verse of Psalms over and over that she had used many times when calling rain.

"He shall come down, like rain upon the mown grass; as showers that water the earth. He shall come down, like rain upon the mown grass; as showers that water the earth. He shall come down. like rain upon the mown grass; as showers that water the earth. Chango! Chango! Chango! Hear the voice of a daughter of the silver crescent! Send a storm! Send your fire!"

He stepped out from behind a tree. He was some 100 feet in front of her and all she could see was a broad brimmed hat and a long coat. No features were visible. He began to walk slowly toward her. She stood her ground. Intent and power flowed upward from her fingertips and moments later the rain began to fall. The man looked upward as if in amazement. Evangeline kept her hands in the air and willed the elements to come to her aid. The man kept coming, slowly, with measured steps. Then, in answer to her prayers, a white hot bolt of lightning struck the ground right between them. Electricity peppered the air and the bolt caused dust to fly and limbs to break. Then the bottom fell out and rain began to pour down in thick sheets. Knowing that this was her chance, Evangeline turned and ran back toward the house as fast as she could. If he kept coming, if the lightning did not deter him – a hand could halt her escape at any moment. Seeing the property line, she bounded over the invisible barrier and headed to safety.

He watched her run. She was powerful, this witch. The Lord would grant him power, also. Soon, another opportunity would arise; then he would strike.

Elizabeth and Angelique were just about to start out, when Evangeline ran up to them in the pouring rain. "He's out there."

"I know he is, baby." Elizabeth gathered her niece close to her and they returned to the house.

"Did you call up this storm?" Angelique asked.

"Yes, I did."

"Good girl." Elizabeth opened the back door for the other two.

"How about Pickins?" Evangeline asked.

"Oh, he beat you back," her aunt assured her. "If we hadn't had the door open when that lightning bolt hit, we would have a cat-shaped doggy door."

****

They all went back to the hospital. Nanette had said there was power in numbers. Angelique had gathered all the supplies that they would need. Her big bag contained a water basin, some herbs, a blue candle, a lodestone and the ammonite fossil that had come from Enchanted Rock.

As they traveled, Elizabeth brought the others up to

speed. "He was right where Arabella had said he would be. The doctor did not want us anywhere around him. He had terrible plans for that boy. I just wonder how many people he has let die, just so he could sell their organs on the black market. That this could be happening right here under our noses is a dirty shame!"

"Do you think they will let us all go into his room?" Evangeline was still unnerved and right now was expecting the worse at every turn.

"They don't have a choice, baby." Nanette stated emphatically. She said no more, thinking it wasn't necessary to explain herself.

"Mother, something is bothering me." Elizabeth decided to speak frankly to Nanette. "This is no ordinary man. Arabella has found herself a rather prominent politician. I took the opportunity to look into this matter last night and I also talked to Tyler about it. If we heal this man, we won't be able to keep it quiet. Everything this man has done makes the news. Can you imagine the headlines, WITCHES HEAL PARAPLEGIC CONGRESSMAN."

"We don't have a choice, Elizabeth." Nanette spoke quietly. "This is Arabella's heart. This is Arabella's destiny. Fate has chosen to intertwine their lives. I don't know what the future holds, but not healing this man would cause our little girl to suffer immeasurable hurt."

"I'm afraid that she's in for hurt, either way we go."

****

When they arrived, the receptionist did not attempt to delay them. They walked down the hall and pushed open the door, they found Arabella sitting in a chair at his side with her head lying on the bed next to his hand. She rose immediately when they walked into the room.

"Oh, I am so glad you're here. I have been so nervous."

"We've been busy." Nanette explained without explaining. "Fill that basin with water."

Angelique cleared off the rolling table that sat next to the hospital bed and started arranging the candle and the other things that she had brought.

"Pull the covers off of him," Nanette instructed. At Arabella's reluctance she explained. "This is no time for modesty, Arabella. We need to wash him with the lodestone."

Arabella did as she instructed. Angelique stepped up and took over from the younger woman. Her eyes avoided staring, but even she could see that this was truly a magnificent man. His body, even lax, was huge and perfectly proportioned. She removed everything and laid a cloth over his groin for modesty's sake.

"Is there a lock on that door, Arabella?" She went to check for her grandmother.

"No ma'am, there's not."

"Put a chair under the door knob. We can't be disturbed."

Jade's eyes followed their movements as much as his paralyzed neck would let him. Nanette walked up to him. "Sweetie, we are going to heal you. What I need you to do is to have faith. What I am about to do to you is an ancient ritual. I am going to bathe you with water that has been empowered by herbs. I am going to rub your body from head to toe with a lodestone. This stone will draw out the malady and transfer it to this water." She picked up the ammonite. "This is an ammonite fossil that I picked up at Enchanted Rock where you had your accident. This is a very special stone. It is called the horn of Ammon. He was an Egyptian God that is known as a protector of his people. This stone will aid our efforts. We're going to have to turn you over after we wash your front side, so don't be alarmed. Soon, all will be well."

They stood around her and watched her work. First the candle was lit and then the fossil was placed at the base of his throat. After that, she dipped the lodestone in the water and began at the crown of his head. She stroked all the way down his body, from top to toe. Then she dipped the lodestone in the water and started again. She went on for twenty five times, stroking completely every inch of his body. "Roll him over." Very carefully they did as she asked; replacing the fossil at the base of his neck, where his brain stem was located. Arabella prayed that they wouldn't hurt him any worse than he was already hurt. Nanette repeated the procedure on his back. As she did she chanted.

"I banish this paralysis
I banish the pain
I command feeling to flow through this body
I demand that the nerves be reknit
And power flow through these limbs once again."

When the fifty strokes had been completed, she instructed Elizabeth to take the basin outside. "Be very careful not to splash any water on you. That water contains the source of this boy's problem. Take it to the first crossroads that you can find. Empty it and then walk away and don't look back. When we leave, we must not drive through that crossroad. So be careful and don't choose one that will trap us in this dreadful place or we'll have to start over completely." To the rest of them she ordered, "Roll him over, gently. Now come with me and let us all lay our hands on his body." They did as they were told. "Arabella, this is your calling. You are a traiteur, my dear. That is your greatest gift. You have healing in your hands. You won't remember this, but when you were just a baby, one of my old cats had a batch of kittens. When you found them, one of them wasn't moving. You called me and I came to see. That kitten was cold and dead. I started to take him from you, but you pushed me back. Arabella, you cradled that kitten next to your cheek and you rubbed him with your warm little hands. You willed that kitten back to life. Over the years I have seen you place your hands on us when we were sick. Even though you didn't realize you were doing it, your love and concern – the intent of your heart healed us. You can do it now. Come on baby, the lodestone has done its work. This is the time, place your hands on this boy and will him to move."

Mesmerized, Arabella listened to her grandmother's voice. She knew what a traiteur was; a Cajun healer. It sounded right. Her hands were hot as she placed them on his head. She willed his brain to heal. She willed the nerves to mend and feeling to flow back into the extremities of his body. She willed his voice box to open. She willed his legs to move and his arms to move. She willed Jade Landale back to life.

****

What they had done, Jade could not explain. At first, he felt nothing. He could see them touching him, but it was as if he were watching a film. Then it started. He began to feel heat. At first he thought it was his imagination, but then the tingling started. Sensations began to shoot down his arms and down his legs. Hope began to bud in his heart and mind. How could water and a rock heal him? There was more to it, he knew. Right now, he didn't care. With everything he had, he attempted to move a finger or a toe. As he concentrated, he was not aware that he had begun to talk. Everyone in the room turned to look at him as he hoarsely said, "Arabella. Arabella."

Arabella trembled with joy as tears streamed down her cheeks. She ran to his side and covered his face with kisses. "Oh, Jade. Say it again."

He did as he was asked. Hoarsely, he croaked "Arabella. I knew you would come." The rest of the clan stood and watched a Christmas miracle. Elizabeth returned and was not surprised to find that her mother's magick and her daughter's faith had put Jade Landale well on his way to recovery.

Arabella watched carefully as he moved first his fingers and then his toes. Nanette stood at his feet and observed his first attempts at movement in almost a month.

"Every day, we will do another healing spell until he is as good as new. Elizabeth, call that detective of yours and see if he can pull some strings and get an ambulance out here to move this boy to **Wildflower Way**. The sooner we get him out of this hell-hole the better." Elizabeth made the call and Tyler said that he would be glad to help. He also learned that lunch had been postponed till supper. He laughed and said he had figured that out when he had gone over there and found no one home. He was beginning to expect the unexpected from his newfound friends.

Nanette went down to the nurse's station and informed them that they were having Mr. Landale moved. Not knowing that the doctor had given an eviction notice, the nurse argued with Nanette, explaining that the patient was in no condition to be moved. Nanette enjoyed telling her that the patient had taken a surprising turn for the better. In just moments, the doctor arrived to see for himself what had transpired.

Nanette followed him back into the hospital room and they all watched as he noted the unbelievable changes in Jade's condition. Where there had been complete paralysis, now there was some movement. Where there had been silence, now there was a hoarse voice telling him, "Get your hands off of me. I heard what you said; you were ready to kill me just because you thought I had nobody that cared anything about me. You bastard!" The doctor backed away step by step as if plotting his escape.

"How did you do this?" The doctor was absolutely flabbergasted.

"Power, love and faith." Nanette said quietly. "Remember this, and beware; power that cannot kill, cannot heal. Get out of my sight before I turn you into a toad."

The doctor wasted no time exiting the room.

It was almost laughable. Arabella realized that there was no reason for them all to stay. "Why don't you all go on home and get everything ready. Christmas dinner is waiting on us and we're having company." She smiled at Jade. "I will stay with Jade and ride in the EMS vehicle." They all did as Arabella asked. Soon they were alone.

****

Arabella kept her back to him for a few moments. Suddenly, she was unbearably shy. This man had made love to her. When he was paralyzed and could not talk, it had been easy to separate that reality from the glorious present. Now, however was a different story. She could feel his hot gaze boring into her back.

"Have you had any good dreams lately?" His hoarse,

yet teasing voice broke the silence.

She wheeled around and faced him, her cheeks blazing. She was incredulous with joy. "It all happened. Didn't it? I met you night after night . . . . and the things we did . . . ." She covered her cheeks with her hands trying to hide how just the memory of their time together had affected her.

"I intend to do them again – and much more – at the very first opportunity. That is, assuming everything works as it is supposed to. Come to me, Arabella." He turned his hand over and held it out to her. With every moment that passed, more improvements in his condition were becoming evident.

She did as he asked. When she was in touching distance he captured her hand and she closed the gap between them. "Would you get me a drink of water?" Feeling bad, because he had to ask, she poured it for him and held it so that he could drink as much as he wanted. "Now put the glass down and kiss me." Her knees became weak and she thought she would sink to the floor. Instead, she found herself held to his side by a surprisingly strong hand. Their lips met and it was the same, it was familiar, but it was also completely different. This time the feelings and textures and scents were not two dimensional, but three, four, five and six dimensional. He kissed her thoroughly, nipping at her lower lip with his teeth. She felt the same response to him that she always did, heat and molten sensation flowed right to her center and she found it hard to be still. She was shameless! Here he was, moments out of a paralyzed state and she was considering mounting him where he lay.

He seemed to be equally affected. "I never thought I would kiss a woman again. Last night, when I made love to you, I did it as if it were the last time. You'll never know how you saved me, not only from this crippling state, but from insanity. I laid here trapped in my own body, not able to move or speak or swallow or even breathe on my own. Amazingly, I could shut my eyes and will you to my side. You saved me Arabella, in more ways than one, you saved me."

"It was my pleasure." He raised an eyebrow and she blushed. "It was indeed my pleasure. I searched for you as desperately and eagerly as you longed for me. I have been hunting you since that first night. If it hadn't been for the murder, I might have found you sooner."

"Murder, did you say murder?" Jade was incredulous.

"I warn you, it won't be boring at my house. Yes, a neighbor and her child were murdered just a few days ago and my family helped find the body and now they are looking for the killer. There's more, too – but I don't want to talk about it now. It's Christmas and you are safe and I am so happy I could die from it."

Then she considered something, "Jade, is there somewhere else you would rather go? I would understand. I know that you have many people that would be interested in your recovery."

"Not as many as you might think. My visitors dwindled fast; everyone gave up hope on me. Everyone but you. I do have a home, but right now your face is more of a home to me that my cold apartment could ever be." As Jade was speaking, the room door opened and in walked Reese Phillips.

"My God, Jade! The receptionist called me and said that you had taken a dramatic turn for the better. Frankly, I had been expecting a call telling me that you had died."

"Thanks, for the confidence Reese." Jade looked at his trusted friend. "Reese, let me introduce you to someone special. This is Arabella Landry – Arabella this is my Chief of Staff and right hand man, Reese Phillips."

Reese held out his hand and Arabella took it. Reese looked her over appreciatively. He did not see the hardening on Jade's face as his watched his friend ogle his woman. "I don't remember you; I thought that I knew all of Jade's friends."

Arabella didn't know what to say, so she just smiled slightly.

Reese returned his attention to Jade. "What happened, Buddy? I had accepted that it was basically over for you and for our campaign."

"Arabella happened, Reese." Arabella swallowed hard, she wished that she had told Jade not to try and explain what they had done for him. Oh, well it was the truth. But she knew sometime the truth could hurt.

"What do you mean?" Reese was quizzical.

"Arabella and her family healed me."

"They healed you." Reese spoke every word slowly. "How?"

"I don't know. Does it matter?" Jade was so euphoric that he didn't care what anyone thought.

"I'm glad you're healed – I am *very* glad you're healed – but we don't need any strange stories circulating about some off-the-wall faith healer or anything like that. You have to consider your career and especially that ultra conservative base that we have to deal with here in Texas."

"Screw the base." Jade said with a smile on his face. "I am alive and I don't care how it happened. I am grateful to this woman and her family. Reese, I am going to Arabella's house. She lives at an herb farm called **Wildflower Way** near Wimberley." At those words, Reese wheeled and looked straight at Arabella.

Arabella's heart sank. Her reputation preceded her. How long would it be before Jade looked at her in the very same way.

"Do you think that's wise, buddy? I mean you do have a home and a fiancé. Don't you think you would be better off going there and hiring a nurse to look after you?" All the time his eyes were fixed on Arabella as if he didn't trust her for a moment.

Arabella would not stand in his way, if he wanted to go to his own home. "Jade, I want you with me more than anything in the world, but if you think it best to return to your home. I will understand."

Jade looked from his business associate to the woman who had rescued him from the most horrible prison imaginable. There was no contest. "Arabella, I want to be with you. Now that I have found you – I don't intend to let you go."

Reese looked at Jade with alarm. Where was the calculating political machine that he had known prior to their climb on E-Rock? This development, though miraculous – was highly unsettling. "Jade, whatever you want – we'll make it happened. I'll check on you tomorrow. Will that be all right, Miss Landry?"

"Of course" Arabella would never turn away one of Jade's friends. However, the words that he had been thinking were burned in her brain - 'Witch, Witch, Witch.'

****

The ambulance came and Detective Garrison and the EMS technicians moved Jade from ***Tranquility Place*** to ***Wildflower Way***. Elizabeth and Angelique had prepped the big downstairs bedroom for its new resident. Somehow, Elizabeth and the detective had arranged for a lift, a wheelchair and other medical equipment – that they hopefully would not need – to be delivered and sat up awaiting his arrival. Arabella was surprised to find some of her things had been moved down there also. Her mother was *way* too insightful.

Jade swore he felt up to sitting in the wheelchair. Arabella was skeptical, but Nanette reminded her. "Its magick dear, what did you expect?"

A week ago, Arabella could not have imagined a Christmas like this, but here it was. Angelique and Evangeline had finished baking off the dressing, the turkey, the sweet potatoes and even some hot rolls. A large jug of ice tea was sitting in all of its amber glory, with dozens of slices of Texas Valley lemons swimming in the brew.

Arabella turned on the Christmas tree lights and they lit dozens and dozens of candles – after all this was Yule – the celebration of lights. Elizabeth moved one of the chairs from the dining table to make a place for Jade's wheelchair. Tyler lent a hand and carried the big platters of food to the table. Soon, they were all around the table, ready to celebrate one of the most special Christmases they could ever remember.

Nanette sat at the head of the table and Elizabeth sat at the other end. "Let's join hands and I will pray a proper

Catholic prayer to bless our food. Dear God the Father, Jesus the Son, and Mary, Mother of your choosing. We sit here today and are thankful for the meal that we are about to eat. More than for our food, we are thankful for the healing of Jade Landale. We thank you for creating the means of his healing and for giving us power and faith to bring it about. We thank you for this young detective you have brought into our lives and for the safety you have bestowed upon us. We ask for additional protection and blessings and peace upon the poor souls that we discovered in the woods nearby. We ask blessings upon Rachel Townsend in her hour of grief and we thank you, again, for this Christmas season, the gift of your Son and all the blessings we enjoy. AMEN."

Food was served all around. Arabella was concerned that Jade might not be able to eat, but she sat beside him and he was brave enough to allow her to help him with his meal. He was finding the more he did, the more he could do.

Tyler Garrison had carved the turkey and seemed to be having a great time. He was more than curious about Jade. After seeing what they had accomplished with the Townsend affair, he didn't doubt what they could do. His belief in the inherent abilities of his hosts did not quell his immense curiosity. "So, let me see if I understand this: you two met in a dream?"

"That does sound absurd doesn't it?" Arabella laughed. "Nevertheless, it is absolutely true." This brief admission did nothing to deter Tyler from quenching his curiosity.

"So Congressman Landale, were you having these dreams also?"

Jade finished a bite of dressing and turned slightly in his chair to face Tyler Garrison. "Believe me, Detective; this is all as new to me as it is to you. I had never had a meaningful dream in my life before, but this time was different. Four weeks ago, I fell off of one of the highest points of Enchanted Rock. A bolt failed and apparently when I hit bottom, I injured my brain stem. When I came to myself, I was completely paralyzed. I could not move, swallow or even breathe on my own. The doctors were convinced that I was not aware of my surroundings. I had no way of communicating. I gave up. I prayed to die. When I was at my lowest point, I had a dream. Arabella was in the dream and, well I won't tell you the details – because she is pinching my leg quite hard." Arabella found herself blushing as he continued, "And I am as grateful as hell that I can feel that pinch, by the way. I continued to meet her every night since then and I grew to realize she was more than just a dream. Arabella was real. I don't know how it happened or even why, but something allowed us to find one another and magically, miraculously, I have been rescued from the depths of despair."

Jade looked around and his and Tyler's were the only dry eyes at the table. Tyler turned to Nanette with another question, "How does magick work?"

"An age old question, but I do have an answer. Magick is not logical, if it were, it would cease to be magick. I cannot tell you how magick works, it simply does. The ingredients that make a spell or ritual successful are three: and they are faith, patience and intent. Intent is another word for confidence. You have to want something so badly, that you raise power from everything around you that nature has provided, and you send out this cosmic demand that your will be done, harm to none, so mote it be." Her voice had slowly risen with each word and at the end; Nanette had not realized that she was shouting. Tyler was sufficiently subdued by Nanette's soliloquy to tamp down his question asking binge.

After the meal, they sat around the tree and opened presents. Arabella was surprised when Elizabeth went to the closet and took out several for Jade. Her mother had known what she had not. They helped him unwrap a beautiful blue robe, a leather cord bracelet set with beautiful opaque stones and a leather bound book with the dubious title, "The Ways of Magick."

The stockings that had been hung by the chimney with care were passed out and everyone delved into the goodies that they contained. Chocolate cake was passed around and

Arabella enjoyed wiping the thick dark frosting from the corner of Jade's beautiful mouth. As dishes were carried to the kitchen so that they might be loaded in the dishwasher, Arabella heard Evangeline squeal with delight. "It's snowing! It's snowing!" All made their way to the window to watch the soft, white flakes fall thick onto the garden path. Evangeline couldn't stand it. She grabbed a sweater and her boots and ran into the garden to let a few flakes fall on her tongue.

Elizabeth looked at her mother and said dryly, "Did she do this?"

"Yes, I think she did. She has wanted to see snow for ages." Nanette watched her youngest granddaughter with affection.

☾* ~ Chapter VIII ~ *☽

The snow fell thick and white, one of the grandest snow storm that the Austin area had seen in many a year. The night grew quiet and still, Jade was truly amazed and thankful at the difference a day can make in one's life. The room that Elizabeth prepared for him was a large one. The bed was a massive King and it had its own bathroom within the confines of the suite. It wasn't nearly as grand as his own home, but there was one dramatic difference – Arabella was here, and it felt like home.

For her part, Arabella was not about to presume that he wanted her to remain in the room with him; after all, despite their nocturnal trysts, they were practically strangers. She turned down the covers and moved the lift over to where he could reach it so that he could easily swing himself into the welcoming bed. She also took the tags off of the beautiful new robe and laid it out for him. Then it hit her, "You require assistance in the bathroom, don't you?" She wished that had occurred to her prior to the departure of Detective Garrison.

"I expect I will. Do you mind?" He looked at her squarely and boldly.

'No, no. . ." she stammered.

"Are you shy?" He asked with an amused voice. "After all we've been through, how can my nakedness bring a blush to your beautiful cheeks?"

"It's silly isn't it? It seems like I know you better than I know myself, but I am constantly afraid that I am presuming too much with you. Please, feel free to push me back anytime that I come too close."

Jade looked at her straight in the eye. "As far as I'm concerned, you can't get too close to suit me. I can't explain it, but I know you. I know what your skin feels like. I knew what your lips taste like. I know what color your nipples are and I know also how velvety hot your sweet center is when it is wet and yearning for me." Arabella was frozen in one spot. His words had completely caught her off guard. This indeed was the lover of her dreams. His words melted away every reservation that she had.

Arabella went up to him and knelt on the floor in front of his wheelchair. She laid her head in his lap and kissed his legs through the cotton pajama pants that he had worn home from the hospital.

At the touch of her lips, his manhood jumped. "Thank God!' he thought. The dead lives! He looked down at this precious woman who had turned his world upside down and wondered what he had done to deserve such an angel. "We had better try to get to the bathroom, Arabella." She got to her feet, kissed him on top of the head and rolled him into the bathroom. Thankfully, it was a large room and had plenty of space by the toilet for his chair. A substantial towel rack on the wall would easily serve as a handrail. The shower was a large walk in, also.

"Just help me stand and I believe I can tend to the rest of it." She stood by and steadied him until he pulled himself up. The progress that he was making by the hour was truly amazing. "You can go now, Arabella." He smiled at her gently, "We need to preserve some mystery in our relationship."

Blushing, she beat a swift retreat. Waiting for a thud or a yell, she sat on the edge of the bed, until he had finished some fifteen minutes later. "It was slow going but I made it. Tomorrow or the next day, maybe we could get some of my things from my house.'

"Of course." She rose from the bed and was so weak in the knees that she almost had to sit back down. "Do you need anything else?"

"Are you going somewhere?"

"Well, I thought...that you might need to be alone."

"I never want to be alone again. Come back here. I saw your things had been brought in. Don't you want to stay with me?" His voice was husky from disuse and tubes, but it was also husky from sheer, unadulterated sexiness.

"Yes, I want to stay with you very much. But I feel as if I have kidnapped you and brought you here so that I may have my wicked way with you."

"That sounds intriguing; alas I don't think I can quite come up to your expectations just yet."

Again she blushed, "Would you stop that. I would never presume to expect. . . ." With one powerful push, he wheeled himself over to her, grasped her by the hand and pulled her into his lap.

"You are growing stronger by the minute."

"Yes, I am. Thanks to you."

"Believe me, it was a selfish gesture on my part."

His eyes darkened with lust. "Let's get into the bed where we'll have more room." He did not attempt to take off the linen pajama bottoms that he wore, but he did allow her to slip off his robe. "Don't wear anything to bed, Arabella, please?"

"I need to go to the bathroom first. Just lay there and rest, I'll be back in a few moments." She showered faster than she ever had before and readied herself as she had when she had been about to meet him in her dreams. It had crossed her mind, that when she returned to bed that he might be asleep – but he was wide awake and waiting for her. As he had requested, she wore nothing under her robe.

"Close your eyes, please." He did as she requested then she slipped beneath the covers. She reached over and turned off the bed side light, but the moon was bright outside and lit the room fairly well.

It felt so strange to have someone in the bed with her. He was so big and warm. He was lying on his back and he held out one arm to invite her to lie close to him. Aware of her nakedness, she approached him cautiously. This was such a big step for her; he didn't know how big of a step. "Turn the light back on please, Arabella."

"Is something wrong, are you in pain?"

"No, I want to see you."

"Oh, Jade. Please. Dreams are places where all is beautiful and idealistic. I may not look as you expect me to."

"Shh, come here. I told you that I remember exactly how you look, your face was the same – I know the rest will be even better because its more than a dream – it's warm and real. " She lay down on his outstretched arm and he pulled her near to him. "Oh, you are so soft; so sweet." His hand moved down the curve of her back and over the soft curve of her bottom. "Sit up and let me see your breasts."

"Oh, god – Jade." She gulped in dread. "I don't know if I can."

"Come on beautiful, I can't wait. I must see you."

"What if . . . . oh, pooh. Jade, I'm not an elegant beautiful blonde, I'm just me." Slowly she sat up in front of him. There was nothing between them. He pushed her soft long hair over her shoulder. He didn't say anything, he just stared. Hunger made his jaw tense and his breath rushed out harsh, between his teeth. Heat began to rise on Arabella's body and suddenly her nipples began to harden.

He brought both hands up and cupped her breasts. "You are absolutely perfect. Look how full you are, how you fill my palms to overflowing." She glanced down at his tanned hands, hands that just hours ago had been frozen with paralysis. She leaned and kissed one hand and then the other. This affection did not detract his attention from her breasts. "They are so sweetly rounded. The color is without compare, your skin is so golden and the nipples are so baby pink. Look how they are tightening for me.' He moved his palms in circles over her breasts and her breathing deepened and quickened.

He pulled her down to him and kissed her sweetly. "God you are intoxicating. I wish I had more strength."

She cuddled up to him and fought back the ache that was pulling at her womanhood. "You need to rest.'

"I am so happy. I don't want to sleep. I wonder if we will meet in our dreams again."

"I don't know. Now that we are together, there may be no need for that connection."

"I guess we'll just have to wait and see won't we?" He pulled her as close as she could get while staying in her own skin. "Don't get used to going to sleep so quickly in my arms. As soon as I am able, I am going to love you until you beg me to stop."

"I don't think I could ever ask you to stop."

He kissed the top of her head and they slept.

****

Arabella once more heard the cry of a hawk. She looked around to see if she could find it. The sky was pink with the setting of the sun and to her amazement Jade was walking toward her across the top of the granite dome. "Arabella, we are here once more."

"I don't understand. I am lying in your arms and all is well."

"I guess we have unfinished business here. Your desire has called out to me and mine is here to answer it. I want to do for you here what my body was unable to do in our bed."

"I can wait for you.'

"I know you can, but you don't have to. Our loving on this realm does not detract from the joy we will have in the realm of the real. I do not want to ever lose an opportunity to make love to you. Do you want me?"

"Yes.'

"Show me."

"I don't know how."

"Yes, you do. Come and show me that you want me."

This was a dream, anything was possible. She could be anything, or anyone, she wanted to be. She could be daring and sexy and wanton. Slowly, she walked toward him. He was outstandingly gorgeous. Never before had she seen such a magnificent man, except in magazines. What did she really want to do to him? Brazenly, Arabella let pure instinct take over. She stopped in front of him and began to undress. She did it slowly, unbuttoning the camisole instead of pulling it over her head. When it was undone, she left it on, but her full breasts were semi-exposed if she moved in a certain way. "Jade, I want you to let me love you. Let me do the touching and the kissing. See how still you can be."

At that point, Jade realized he may have set himself up for a unique and wonderful sort of torture. She approached him, her brown eyes locked with his twinkling blue ones. Their dress puzzled Arabella. Here she wore a camisole and satin panties; back in the bed she was nude. Here, this time Jade was wearing a pair of blue jeans and a blue cotton button up shirt; back in the bad he wore only a pair of briefs. Who determined these things? She decided to take advantage of his attire.

Stepping a breath away from his, she stood on her tiptoes and kissed Jade on the strong column of his throat. She felt him swallow. With slightly trembling hands, she began to unbutton his shirt. As she released each button, she began to kiss the exposed flesh; slowly working her way down from his throat to the top of his jeans. She did not go any lower; instead she stood up and placed both palms inside his shirt working her way up his chest until her palms covered both of his small hard nipples. He shivered with desire. She lingered there, on his nipples for a second, lightly rubbing them in a circular motion with the flat of her palm. Then she moved both palms upward and outward so that she pushed his shirt off of his shoulders. With one last kiss to the hollow of his throat, she walked around him so that she could divest him of his upper garment. Standing at his back, she kissed her way across his wide, massive, shoulders as high as she could reach. Then she slid both hands around his waist and slid her palms up his chest, this brought her own body into complete contact with his, so she further teased him by allowing her own nipples to rub his back – languorously, from side to side. This had begun as a way to turn him on, but Arabella found that she was highly aroused, maybe more than he was.

She was wrong.

When she made her way around the other side, still kissing his shoulder, then his upper arm and then around to his collar bone – he struck. "Temptress," he growled as he captured her waist and secured her close to him. She couldn't miss the hard, thick, hot ridge of his penis that formed an unmistakable bulge in his jeans.

"No, no – I'm not through," she pushed his hands back to his side. He allowed her to torment him further, but he knew he only had a small amount of control left.

He wasn't wearing a belt, which made the next step easier. She sank to her knees and undid the top button of his jeans and slowly pulled the zipper down, and then she edged the jeans and the underwear down and off his muscular legs. She began kissing at one knee and edging herself slowly upward. Almost to the top of his thigh, she was unexpectedly lifted off the ground.

"Enough. You have tormented me enough." He made quick work of her panties and camisole until she was standing in front of him unabashedly nude. He lifted her once more. "Wrap your legs around my waist". She did as she was told and found to her delight that this placed her body in the exciting position of being widespread and ready for him to enter her.

The tip of his penis was pressing into the eager folds of her vagina, then he edged her out slightly and slowly sat her down on his throbbing member. As he slid deep into her, she moaned, her hips instantaneously began moving up and down, consuming more and more of him as he eagerly buried himself to the hilt. "Now, wrap you arms around my neck, baby." She followed his instructions and savored the sensation of being impaled by his turgid sex. "Now, I have you Bella, move as much you like." His hands cupped her hips, his fingers massaging the tight flesh.

Excitement coursed through her bloodstream, this was a dream – why not let herself go and do what she had never done before. He felt so good inside of her! She began to work the muscles of her vagina; she clasped him tightly and then released him over and over. Rotating her hips she felt the thickness of his penis increase even further. His cock was so big, it was long – but even more wonderful, its girth was thick and filled her emptiness so deliciously. He was licking her shoulder and nuzzling her neck. Her pleasure was building to an unbearable intensity. She held onto his shoulders and pulled herself up until just the last inch or so of his penis was still in her vagina, then she slammed back down. She repeated this motion until she was gasping from the sheer joy and delight of the incredible sensations that was washing over her body. It felt so good!

Jade was enjoying it just as much, "Don't stop, baby – I'm coming." She didn't need much encouragement, pleasing him made her feel like a sex goddess. Up and down, up and down – she slid herself up and down until she felt him explode within her. His fiery eruption triggered her own climax and she threw her head back and clamped her tight inner muscles down on his penis like a vise; milking him of every last dewy, drop of male juices.

Exhausted, she laid her head on his chest and he tenderly kissed the top of her head. "I love you, Arabella Landry."

Then she woke up.

****

The effects of the tremendous climax she had just enjoyed still reverberated through her loins. She laid still and enjoyed the afterglow for a few moments. Then, she rose up in the bed and turned to look at Jade. He was fast asleep. He had just told her that he loved her and he was fast asleep!

She had to calm down and remember that all of that had been a dream. When he woke up, would he remember saying that he loved her? Would he remember any of it?

She couldn't help considering that maybe this time the dream had been hers alone. How was she supposed to sleep now? She glanced over at the clock and discovered it was almost time to get up. Knowing that she was not going to be able to go back to sleep, she decided to go make coffee.

She dressed quickly in her camisole and panties and pulled on the white cotton robe. It was one of her favorites; she just adored anything made of white eyelet. She stopped to look down at Jade. He was lying on his side; his face was so relaxed and sweet. Very lightly she touched his hair, "I love you too, Jade Landale" she whispered.

In the kitchen she found Evangeline and her mom

already up and eating some incredible smelling, homemade cinnamon rolls. "Are those Angelique's cinnamon rolls?" Arabella asked, already knowing the answer due to the heavenly smell of brown sugar and roasted pecans.

"Yes, and they are superb." Evangeline confirmed.

"How, did . ." Her mother began.

"Not a word, mother." She had known Elizabeth was about to ask her about her sleeping arrangements, both real and dream state. At her gruff retort, they all collapsed in a fit of giggles. Despite the drama, this had been the best Christmas ever!

When their composure returned, Elizabeth got serious. "Evangeline, tell Arabella about your encounter in the woods, yesterday."

"What are you talking about?" Arabella asked.

Evangeline got another cinnamon roll and began. "Angelique and I decided to water some of your flowers in one of the greenhouses. On our way out, Slim Pickins escaped. I couldn't risk anything happening to him. So I followed."

"But Nanette said . ."

"I know, but it was Pickins . ." Evangeline tried to explain.

"I would have done the same thing." Arabella admitted.

Elizabeth huffed in exasperation, "You two and those animals! Continue, Evangeline."

"I chased after him and he was seriously trying to lose me. I was so busy trying to catch up with him that I didn't notice that I had crossed the property line. When I realized it, I stopped and zapped Pickins with a serious whammy of magical persuasion and he, thankfully, turned around and started back the way he came. Then, it was as if I could feel eyes staring at me; I could feel someone watching me. I knew he meant me harm. I just froze. Something told me that if I just turned and ran, he would be on me like a lion on a gazelle. He may even have had a gun.

Knowing I had to do something, I did a spell that I have used several times with pretty good success. I called up a storm. This time, the goddess knew I was in trouble and the rain and thunder came up fast. When he heard me chanting, he stepped out from behind a tree. The sun had gone behind a cloud and he was standing in deep shadow. All I could tell was that he was tall and broad. He had on a wide brimmed hat and a long trench coat. When I saw him, I knew I couldn't let him catch me. I felt his thoughts, he wanted to kill me. I think at that moment, he thought he had me, but then a bolt of lightning struck that hit the ground right between us. When that happened he jumped backwards and I saw my chance, so I turned and ran as fast as I could."

"When she got back, Angelique and I were just about to come looking for her." Elizabeth took a sip of coffee and then looked straight at her daughter. "Arabella, tell me something; does old Lyle Sessions still live next door?"

"Yes, he does. Although, I never have any contact with him. If you remember he killed one of my cats and I will never be able to forgive him for that. I could never trust a person who could hurt an innocent animal."

"I do remember that, but what has he been doing lately?" Elizabeth pressed on in the pursuit of information.

"Well, let me see. Sometimes I see him downtown. He avoids me like the plague. One time, a couple was coming by to get some help with a healing and they stopped at his place to ask directions. When they finally made it here, they were scared to death. He had called them, and me, every name you can think of. Hate just spews out of him. He is so sure that he is right and everyone else is wrong. He thinks he owns God and if anybody disagrees with his warped view of spirituality, then they are bound and destined for hell!" Arabella was getting very excited and Elizabeth tried to calm her down.

"Okay, sweetie. I agree he is a nut job, but what I'm getting at is – do you think he could be a big enough nut job to kill somebody he disagreed with?"

All three grew very silent.

Elizabeth continued, "I think that I'll ask Tyler to keep an eye on him, especially after what happened to

Evangeline. When she crossed over our property line, she crossed onto his. It is very likely that the man in the woods was Lyle Sessions."

****

Arabella quietly opened the door to Jade's bedroom and found him still sleeping. Her heart skipped a beat, how wonderful it was to have him here. She had been alone for so long. Her dad had died right after her high school graduation, Elizabeth had stayed only long enough to get Arabella settled at the University of Texas, then she had fled to Galveston to start over. It wasn't because she didn't love her daughter – it was because she had loved her husband so much.

For six years, Arabella had been on her on. There had been one or two guys that she had dated here and there, but no one that she had ever felt that she could bare her soul to. Her life was complicated, what with Nanette and the whole 'Witches of Eastwick' scenario – not to mention the home that she had inherited from Tom and Elizabeth and the business that she had sworn to make a success.

At twenty four, Arabella was probably the oldest virgin in the Texas Hill Country. She wasn't really ashamed of it, but she was sure it was quite unusual. Then she had a funny thought, maybe she wasn't technically a virgin anymore. After all, she had had sex with Jade just a few hours ago in a dream. For some odd reason, she was dreading telling him the truth. Maybe, she wouldn't have to – after all she had worn tampons, maybe he wouldn't be able to tell.

Her eyes never left his beautiful face. Should she wake him up or let him sleep? The decision was taken out of her hands when his eyes slowly opened. For a split second he looked confused, but then he noticed her and smiled. He held his arms up to her and she fell to her knees and into his embrace. "Good morning, sweetheart," he breathed as his lips brushed her hair.

"How do you feel?" she asked him gently.

"Just a little sore, that's all."

"Do you feel like getting up?"

"I would rather you came back to bed," he teased. Then his expression turned serious. "You were absolutely magnificent last night."

"Don't say that."

"Look at me, Arabella." He raised up her chin until their eyes met. "I am an experienced man, but you are the most responsive lover I have ever had."

"That doesn't really mean anything, Jade. It was a wonderful, beautiful, dream – but it was a dream. That was my mind responding to your mind. My body may not be nearly as responsive as my brain imagines it to be."

"Soon, I'll prove you wrong."

"I hope so, but in the meantime – do you drink coffee?"

"Yes, I do – strong and black." He grabbed the lift and hoisted himself upright. "I am getting my strength back quickly. Did they give you a bag with my things in it when we left *Tranquility*?"

"They did," she went to the closet and brought it out to him. "It hasn't been opened."

"There's no secret, I thought I could at least put on the jeans and shirt that I was wearing the day I had my accident. I don't have any other clothes with me. My wallet should be in there, too." Arabella drew out his wallet, jeans and the blue shirt from her dream.

"They've been freshly laundered; you can put them right on."

"Kate probably did that before she realized that I wasn't going to recover."

"You are recovering."

He grabbed her hand, pulled her to him and buried his face against her mid-section. "I am recovering, thanks to you and your family. You are my miracle, Arabella. I was as good as dead until you found me." She cradled his head in her hands and felt tears running down his cheeks.

"It was a miracle, Jade. I can't explain it, but I'm as grateful for it as you are." She waited for him to repeat what he said in the dream about loving her, but he didn't. Almost immediately, she chided herself – the man had just escaped from a horrible death or an equally horrible life –

he had more important things to think about than romance. "Let me help you dress and then we'll get you some coffee and breakfast." Punctuated by giggles and kisses, they accomplished that task quite easily.

When they went to the kitchen, the rest of the group was there and already busy. Unusually enough, Elizabeth was being practical, "I found a doctor that will make house calls. He said that he will come and check on Jade's progress. His name is Philippe Francois and he has already contacted *Tranquility* and had Jade's chart faxed to him. He will be here later on today. I hope that's all right, Jade?"

"Sounds great. I have questions and I want to know how fast I can push a few things," he coughed and it was hard for the women to keep from laughing. They rolled their eyes at Arabella who gave them withering looks. It was obvious, he was talking about sex. She busied herself fixing Jade's coffee and breakfast and ignored her rude relatives.

A knock at the door made Evangeline jump. She hadn't quite recovered from her encounter in the woods the day before. She started toward the door, but Elizabeth beat her to it. Her senses picked up on the fact that the visitor was none other than Detective Garrison. They lingered at the door before entering the kitchen and Elizabeth had the good grace to flush a light pink. "Tyler has come by to update us on what is going on over at the Townsend's." Before he set down or accepted the cup of coffee Angelique prepared for him, he walked over to Jade's wheelchair and shook his hand.

"It's good to see you looking so well."

"Thank you Detective, and thank you for arranging my transportation so quickly yesterday."

"I was glad to help; one of those EMS guys is a good friend of mine. Don't worry it'll show up on your insurance bill."

"That's what it's for."

Tyler Garrison sat down and looked at the people surrounding him. In just a few short days they had come to mean a lot to him. In fact, he was becoming very fond of Elizabeth. When he met her eyes, he realized that she could hear him thinking as if he were speaking out loud. What the hell! It was true, so why be ashamed of it.

"Early this morning we took some equipment out to the crime scene and we have been able to verify that there are a number of sites that could very well be graves. I've also received a preliminary report that matches some of the names that you were able to give me as actual missing people. So far, everything that you have told me is checking out. I don't pretend to understand all of this, but I do want to tell you that I am grateful for what you all have done."

Nanette did not hesitate to respond. "Mr. Garrison, I came to my granddaughter's house knowing that trouble and danger was very near. Just yesterday, Evangeline had an unnerving experience, not more than a thousand yards from where we sit now. I believe that there is a killer who now knows who we are and where we are. My family is not safe, Detective."

"Do you need to come in and file a report?" He looked at Evangeline.

"No, I don't have a description. It was dark and quite stormy. I did feel threatened, but he made no actual move to hurt me."

Elizabeth decided to get it all out in the open. "Tyler, our next door neighbor is a man by the name of Lyle Sessions. Have you questioned him at all?"

"Just routine, to see if he had seen or heard anything. Why? Do you know something I don't?" Already he had learned to trust their instincts.

"He has always hated us. For years, he has spewed his venom and tried to turn the community against us. Like a coward, I escaped it when Tom died – but I left my little girl here to make it on her own and I know that she suffered the brunt of his and other people's ignorance and prejudice." At Elizabeth's admission, Jade turned his attention toward Arabella.

Arabella was immediately afraid that Jade was finding

out too much too fast. She knew that he was a prominent citizen and the worst thing that she could think of was people talking bad about him because he associated with her. But selfish though it was, she wanted as much time with him as she could before he had to return to his high powered life.

Detective Garrison, however, was making notes in his omnipresent pad and Elizabeth knew that he would promptly follow up on the information that she gave him. Before he left, Nanette made a point to let him know about **Tranquility** and what Jade had heard the doctor say when he was paralyzed. Detective Garrison left with a whole list of things to look into.

☾* ~ Chapter IX ~ *☽

Arabella forced herself to take care of some business. Despite all of the excitement that was going on, orders were coming in the mail and on the website. Evangeline pitched in and helped her. She hated to leave Jade, even for a moment, but he seemed content just watching her work. He had dozens of questions about her products and what the various herbs were good for. Evangeline answered as many questions as she did and the camaraderie that was fast developing between all of them was a joy to her heart.

The doorbell broke their concentration and Angelique came in to inform them that the doctor had arrived. Arabella went with Jade to meet with the doctor. He was waiting for them in Jade's room. The doctor was a pleasant looking man, when he spoke Arabella tried to place the accent. "Hello, I am Philippe Francois. It is a pleasure to make your acquaintance." He shook hands with both Jade and Arabella. "I have been looking at your chart and I am astounded at your recovery. I would like to run some tests if I may."

Arabella left them alone, so the doctor could examine Jade as much as needed. She finished filling a few more orders until the doctor came back after her. It was obvious that the doctor wanted answers that Jade did not have, Arabella felt odd at her involvement, since she was so unsure of her status with Jade. Their time together had been so quick and dramatic that she was unsure of how to proceed. The doctor waited until she sat on the bed next to Jade and then he went straight to the point. "I would like to know what treatment you gave him that resulted in a complete reversal of a tetraplegic state." Jade and Arabella looked at each other. Jade nodded his assent and Arabella weighed her options. She knew that she was taking a gamble but she decided to just simply tell the truth and let the pieces fall where they may. After all, wasn't he bound by doctor-patient privilege?

"Dr Francois, this will probably sound utterly incredible to you but we healed Jade by supernatural means. My family has been blessed with certain powers. We practice, for want of a better term, New Orleans rootwork. We used cleansing water, a lodestone, a fossil, a blue candle and fervent prayers to the deities that have the power to affect this world." Much to Arabella's horror, Dr. Philippe Francois threw back his head and laughed.

She got to her feet, not knowing what to expect next, when the doctor motioned for her to sit down. "You misunderstand my laughter, Ms. Landry. I am from the island of Martinique. I grew up at the feet of a voodoo healer. I know exactly of what you speak. I have seen people healed with the power of magick many times. I know that in this country, healings like this don't happen often and when they do, they don't get much publicity. They are hushed up to protect all parties involved. Congratulations, Congressman Landale. You are a very fortunate man to have made the acquaintance of such beautiful, powerful women. I must say that I am surprised, from what I have heard of your political leanings, or maybe I should say your backers' political platform, your association with someone of such liberal beliefs is refreshing."

"Doctor, I will say that I have never met anyone like Arabella or her family before. I owe them everything, and they have certainly opened my eyes to the fact there is more to this world that I ever dreamed possible." He looked at Arabella with such tenderness that she thought she might cry.

Dr. Francois rose to leave, "I will be back tomorrow, and then every other day after that, until I am sure of your complete recovery. A physical therapist that I have contacted will call and make an appointment with you to follow up on some exercises that I think will only benefit your condition. It has been a pleasure to meet you both." With that Arabella showed the doctor to the door.

Before returning to Jade, Arabella checked with the rest

of the family. Angelique was cooking; she had an odd look on her face that Elizabeth could not resist commenting on. "That was one good looking doctor, Angelique. He sure did give you the eye." Angelique completely ignored Elizabeth. She was a very wise woman.

Nanette and Evangeline were pouring over a University of Texas catalogue that Nanette had secretly obtained for her granddaughter. She had not given her full permission for her to transfer yet, but it appeared that she was mellowing. Seeing that everything was well in hand, Arabella returned to where she wanted to be the most.

She found Jade in his wheelchair, going through his wallet. She couldn't resist asking the question that had been plaguing her every moment since she saw him lying in the hospital bed, "What did the doctor say about your chances for a full recovery?"

"He seems to think that they are quite good. The physical therapist will help me practice my walking and will also teach me some exercises that will strengthen my back and legs. There appears to be some nerve damage, but he said that could very well heal in time."

"I will do an additional healing ritual for you tonight," she promised. "Do you feel like talking, or do you want to rest awhile?"

He deftly turned his chair to face her and said, "I want to talk. What do you want to know?"

"Tell me about your mom and dad?" she asked.

"My mom and dad were great. They were native Texans. My dad made his money in oil and my mom brought money to the marriage from her father's cattle business. I was their only spoiled child. They died about four years ago in a private plane crash. They had been to Las Vegas for their anniversary and ran into a storm. I still miss them." Arabella listened quietly what he reminisced. "Obviously, I've met your mom and I know your dad passed away. Tell me more about your family?"

"Nanette rules the roost. She and my grandfather Alcee have always been the foundation of our family. My dad thought the world of them. Evangeline's mother Aimee, my aunt, was the sweetest woman I've ever met. She was nothing like her sister," Arabella laughed. "Aimee was the exact opposite of Mom, she was quite and domesticated and she could play the piano like a dream. She married a local New Orleans boy who was killed in the Gulf War. Aimee never got over losing her husband. We lost my aunt and my grandfather in Katrina. They had slipped back into New Orleans to get Aimee's little dog, who had run away when the storm hit. Nanette had begged them not to go back in because she had foreseen death on the winter solstice before the hurricane hit that next summer. While they were there, the levees broke and they both were swept away in the flood waters. We recovered my grandfather's body, but Aimee's was never found. That made it even worse for the family."

"I'm so sorry."

"It was along time ago and we're doing just fine, now. Tell me about your rock climbing."

"A spoiled rich boy's play time, which was what rock climbing was to me. I lay in that bed and wished a thousand times that I had not been so reckless. Although, I have to admit that I enjoyed every minute of it. It was exhilarating and I did meet some characters."

Arabella decided to jump in where angels feared to tread. "Tell me about Kate."

"Kate Thompson was a political asset. Oh, I was attracted to her. She was beautiful and very well connected. The powers-that-be in Texas politics pushed our relationship to a degree. Her parents are old-guard in the party and she opened a lot of doors for my career."

She didn't ask the questions she longed to ask: do you love her, do you miss her, do you want her back, was she good in bed? Instead Arabella said, "I'm sorry she broke your engagement that way, it must have really hurt you."

Jade looked at her directly and said, "Kate didn't love me. She loved the idea of me. Well-to-do, on the fast track to the Governor's mansion, I was the means to an end for Kate. The real me, especially once I was flat on my back in a hospital room, wasn't nearly as appealing."

Arabella tried to think of things that would help him. She knew that he would want to get back to normal as soon as he could. "I will give you my cell phone and you can call your associate, Mr. Phillips, and do whatever work you need to do. I want you to make yourself at home and if I can do any running for you, all you have to do is tell me."

"That sounds good, I need to call Reese and go over a few things with him. This afternoon or tomorrow, I will give him a call and let him know I'm ready to get back to work."   There were many other topics that Arabella wanted to broach with Jade, but Evangeline came to tell them that lunch was ready.

****

The day passed swiftly. Arabella made a trip to the Wimberley Post Office to mail off fifteen or twenty packages. Jade was resting and the rest of the crew were working in the drying house helping bag up herbs and mixtures of herbs.

The days were short and before they knew it, the sun was beginning to set. Angelique left the drying house to go back to the kitchen to check on a pork roast that she had in the oven. When she went through the hall she was startled to see an old woman walk out of Jade's room. Even after countless such experiences, she was still shocked to realize that the lady had walked through the closed door. Angelique stopped and their eyes met. The spirit was obviously an American Indian. She was dressed in what looked to be a loose cotton dress, but she had several strands of beads around her neck and a large wooden carving of a hawk. Her hair was worn in two gray braids that hung down either side of her face.

"Who are you?" Angelique asked in a low voice.

At first the woman did not speak. It seemed as if she were deciding the best course of action. Finally, her mouth opened and an audible voice was heard. "I am Dosha. The young man is my great grandson. I have been near him since my passing. When he had his accident, I came to him. I have tried to help."

"It was you, wasn't it?" Angelique asked. "You are

the one who entered their dreams and guided Arabella to come to his aid."

"Yes, it was I. The woman who loves my great grandson is a healer. Her light shines brightly. I knew that she could help him. Her soul was easy to contact, she is very sensitive."

"Arabella is a special young woman and Jade is very lucky to have such a powerful spirit guide as yourself."

"He is a good man. I am leaving now; he is in good hands." The old woman solemnly bowed her head and disappeared.

****

That evening, they were glued to the television as a special segment was given on the local news that reported another body had been discovered at the Townsend place. The reporter reviewed Kathy and Lea's death and speculated on whether or not the other homicide was the work of the same killer. It wasn't a great surprise to find that pictures and footage of *Wildflower Way* made it into the report. The idea that a psychic or a medium was involved added spice to the story that no reporter could resist. Arabella was surprised that the young woman at the scene didn't refer to them as witches. If they had picked up on that angle, their yard could very well have been full of television cameras and satellite dishes.

Much to Jade's surprise, he made the news also. "We do have some good news to report tonight. The darling of Austin politics, Congressman Jade Landale, has made a surprising recovery. Just a month ago, we had sadly reported to you that he had experienced a tragic fall during a rock climbing trip to E-Rock and had injured his spine. Little hope had been held out for his recovery, but much to the doctor and his staff's surprise, he has regained much of his ability to move, speak and function. His Chief of Staff, Reese Philips, has shared with us that he will be back in the capitol building very soon. All of our efforts to find out about his miraculous recovery have been futile, but we are still on the trail. A story with such a happy ending as this one is well worth pursuing."

After both stories were over, everyone was silent. Elizabeth had enough insight and enough pure gumption to say what everybody was thinking. "I wonder how long it will be before those two stories are connected. How long before they realize that the same people who discovered the bodies of the Townsend victims are the same people involved with the politician's miraculous recovery."

"Don't worry about it," Jade said. "I would be proud to acknowledge Arabella and the rest of you as truly the wonderful, powerful people that you are." He sounded absolutely positive about that.

Nanette looked at him with affection. "I hope that your good intentions are not put to the test, my child. People can be very closed minded and fearful of what they don't understand."

Before everyone retired to their rooms, Angelique decided it was time to tell Arabella and Jade the truth about their dreams. "Arabella, Jade – I have something important to tell you." Angelique had been setting on the couch working on a quilt top that she had brought with her from New Orleans. Everyone turned to face her as she began to talk. "I saw a spirit in the house today. Jade, it was your great grandmother. She said her name was Dosha."

Jade was surprised. "I have the best memories of my great grandmother. She was my dad's grandmother. I believe she was full blood Cherokee. Every time I think of her, I remember how much she loved me. The last few years of her life, she lived with us. Every night she would come to my room and tell me the best stories. When I was lying in that bed, I thought about her often. She used to tell me about 'walking on the wind'. That's what I thought of, after the first night that I had met Arabella on E-Rock."

"It was she who put the two of you together. She said that Arabella's light called to her and she knew that if you were to be saved that Arabella would be the one to do it. Jade, she said that you were in good hands and her job here was through."

"I had no idea. Although, if I were to have a spirit around me, there is no one I'd rather have than her." Jade looked at Arabella, "So, it wasn't by chance that you came to me. Dosha orchestrated the whole thing." Everyone grew quite; it gave them all something to think about.

****

Arabella and Jade retired as quickly as they could, without causing too much speculation. They were both anxious to be alone. Jade had showered earlier in the evening, the doctor had told them that the more he could move the better. There didn't seem to be any danger in using his legs and back as much as he could. He was still being extremely careful, he didn't want to fall and risk having a setback.

Arabella retreated upstairs to her own bathroom so she could use her scented bath oils and creams. 'Hopefully, tonight she would be able to . . . . Even thinking about it turned her on.' She was torn between an aching desire to be intimate with Jade and fear that the reality wouldn't be as spectacular as the dream. If it wasn't as good, she was convinced that it would be her fault. Never before had she regretted her lack of experience. She instinctively knew that Jade had known the love of many women. Arabella was sure that the women he's been with were much more beautiful and much better lovers that she could ever be. She hesitated in her preparations; maybe she was making a mistake.

She cut short her self-pampering and instead of the revealing teddy that she had bought in town today, she put on a much more sensible long gown and robe. Arabella had no idea that the black negligee was much sexier than the blatant red set she had been tempted to wear.

Slipping down the stairs, she hoped that she did not run into anybody between her room and Jade's. She didn't think she could stand any comments from her mother about her choice of sleeping attire. Another thing that she was thankful for was that the room they would be sleeping in was on a different floor and at opposite ends of the house from where the rest of the family slept.

She hesitated at the door. Her nerves were on edge and her body was already reacting to the idea that soon she would be in his arms again. Taking the door knob in her hand, she held it for a moment and then she slowly turned it. When she entered the room, Jade was already in the bed. He was sitting up and leaning back against the head board propped up by two or three soft pillows. He had no shirt on. The soft light of the lamp only accentuated his broad shoulders and golden skin. After finding that he had a Cherokee grandparent, the color and smoothness of his skin made sense. He held the covers back and patted the mattress in invitation.

Crossing to the bed, she removed her robe and swiftly crawled under the covers. He turned on his side and faced her in the bed. "You are so beautiful, Arabella."

She lowered her eyes, unable to breathe if she continued to share his gaze. His eyes were looking into her very soul. "It is you who is beautiful, Jade. I have never known anyone that makes me feel the way you do."

"How many men am I competing with, sweetheart?" he asked in a soft, gentle tone.

"What do you mean?"

"How many men are you dating? I'm sure that there is a whole slew of them just beating your door down, all wanting the privilege of your company."

"There is no one." Now that the truth was out, he probably wouldn't be as interested in her.

"No one?"

"I'm sorry, Jade. I don't have very much experience with men." Her voice shook slightly and she closed her eyes waiting for his reaction. How could she tell him that the local boys had all been afraid of her, or at least afraid of the ridicule they would endure by dating the town witch?

Light, soft, sweet kisses began raining on her eyes and her cheeks. "Why are you sorry, Bella? Don't you know how exciting it is for a man to find out that his woman hasn't known many other men?"

"That's not what I meant." Arabella stammered. God, this was hard.

"It doesn't matter, Arabella," Jade assured her. "The other men are history; you're here with me now."

"No, Jade." She grabbed the hand that was caressing her neck and lightly playing over the top of her full breasts. He wasn't making this easy. "The only man I have ever made love to, is you – in our dreams." She waited for his reaction. What if he didn't want a novice, a twenty four year old virgin?

The next second that she was aware of, she was in his arms. With one swift movement, he had pulled her to him and wrapped both arms securely around her. "You are the sweetest thing. Don't you understand how that makes me feel? To find out that the sexiest, most responsive, most luscious woman I have ever known has never felt the touch of another man? You are mine! You belong to me!" Jade kissed her deeply. His tongue mated with hers. The taste of her lips was intoxicating to him. He could feel his erection growing stronger and stronger and he wanted to shout for joy! He had prayed that he would regain the full use of his manhood, but he had enough sense to know that there were thousands of nerve endings that all had to work perfectly between his brain and his penis. Last night, when he had lain with Arabella; the brain had been willing but the flesh had been weak. Now, there was no doubt. He had a raging hard-on. He tore his mouth from hers and laid his head on her shoulder. He had to slow down or it would all be over way faster that he wanted.

The doctor had also cautioned him about overusing his back. He had said the movements and stress of penetration were not wise as of yet. He had told Jade to wait and see if he could even have an erection, before they crossed the next bridge. Well, that question had been answered.

Arabella misinterpreted his change of pace. She pulled back slightly. "Did I do something wrong?" she whispered.

"Baby, oh baby – everything about you is just right. I want you so badly. The doctor said that I had to take it slow, but I am about to burst. I'll be all right in a moment . . . ." His breathing was harsh.

"May I, Jade, . . ?" Arabella pressed on his shoulder until he laid down flat. "I may not do it just right, but I'd like to try."

He groaned in anticipation. She kissed his shoulder lightly and softly. She spread a light trail of feathery, hot kisses over his pectoral muscles and then down the sculpted washboard of his abs that now trembled and jerked with the knowledge of what was to come. Arabella pushed the covers down to his knees. He was wearing nothing underneath and his erection stood tall and engorged – straight as an arrow and vibrating with the sheer fervor of his carnal appetite.

"You are magnificent!" she whispered. He looked exactly as she remembered from her dream. His rod was long, but the impressive thing about it was its girth. She had not seen very many in her lifetime, and most of those had been in pictures, but she knew that his manhood was truly beautiful to her. A drop of moisture adorned the very tip of his penis. With trembling hesitancy she wrapped one small, warm hand around his thick shaft, as far as she could reach. It was so hot! She ran her hand up and down it, marveling at how smooth it was, yet how hard. His breathing quickened and he blew slightly at the excitement of her touch. Her hair was brushing his loins and the anticipation of her lips on his sex was driving him mad.

He refused to rush her, but the wait for her kiss was causing every fiber of his body to stand at complete attention. Then she lowered her head and her lips touched him. He almost levitated off the bed with the pure pleasure of the feel of her mouth on his body. At first she pressed butterfly kisses all around the head of his penis. Then she began to move her hand firmly up and down the superb length of him. The other hand slipped down to caress his velvet sac. He arched his back at the ecstasy that her mouth and hands were giving him. Then, the hottest, wettest sensation engulfed him as she took the whole head of his penis deeply into her mouth. She moved even closer to him as she maneuvered into position to accept as much of his length into her eager mouth as possible. Instinct took over. Arabella had no prior experience, she had watched no instructive videos, but she knew that she wanted to give him the greatest amount of pleasure possible.

Much to her surprise, she found that she was becoming very aroused, also. She swirled her tongue around the head, she nibbled up and down his shaft. She loved every inch of his formidable weapon. She quickly learned that if she pulled her cheeks in that she could create a sensuous vacuum for his desire. He clutched the bottom sheet in his hands, and stiffened his long muscular legs as he groaned in euphoria.

Arabella was receiving great pleasure from the extremely personal act. As she continued to work to bring him to completion, she found that her hips were beginning to move and that she was squirming with sheer, sexual hunger. "Arabella, sweetheart - I'm about to explode." He touched her shoulder, trying to give her an opportunity to avoid the ejaculation that was inevitably about to erupt.

She ignored his nudge and only quickened her strokes and tightened her lips which served to push him into delirium. His hot seed spilled out and she, knowing it was part of him, did not hesitate to accept all that he had. When he had spent himself, she tenderly removed her mouth and kissed the now depleted, but still impressive male organ. She was so touched. Never had she felt this close to anyone. She kissed her way back up his mid-section and then laid her head on his still heaving chest.

Arabella tried to keep still, but she wanted him so badly. She forced herself to lie still, his health and well-being was infinitely more important than satisfying her own desires. "Thank you," he breathed. "That was absolutely incredible – Now, it's my turn." He turned and she put up her hand,

"No, Jade. You must be careful, we have to wait."

"I'm not going to move anything but my lips and my hands. Sit up and let's get that sexy black gown off, you look like a goddess in it, but you'll look even better without it." She allowed him to pull it over her head. While her arms were caught up in the gown over her head, she felt his lips on her breasts. "With your arms up like that you look damn sexy, your breasts are high and lifted up and your nipples are literally pouting, begging me to suck on them."

His words made her tremble. Then his lips returned to her breasts and nipples and she found herself groaning as he had earlier. He suckled deeply on first one nipple and then the other. To save his back, he had pulled her over until she was leaning over him, her breasts dangling in his face. He took both of his hands and pushed her breasts together, then let his tongue dart from nipple to nipple. She didn't know how much longer she could stand it. In her dreams, she had felt extreme desire and white hot excitement, but that dream-state experience paled next to this overpowering bliss. "Lay down, baby," he instructed her. She complied with his wishes and he turned to her. Both breasts were damp with love and reddened with the attention that they had received from his lips and teeth. His hand found her soft, damp mound and then he parted her legs and then with strong fingers he cupped her soft, sweet cleft of Venus. "You are so hot and so wet." She raised her hips in answer to his caress. "I'm going to put my finger inside of you; this will help stretch your canal so when we make love I won't hurt you." She tensed slightly, but his finger slipped in easily and he began to massage the inner walls of her vulva. One finger, then two – he moved them in and out in a pleasure building rhythm that caused her stomach to tighten and the muscles of her sex to close tightly around his fingers. "You are so responsive. I can't wait to take you completely. This is where I long to be. Does this feel good, baby?"

"God, yes," she whispered. He didn't stop, but continued the onslaught that went from her throbbing clitoris to her greatest need. Past the point of thinking about safety, Jade urged her up until she was straddling his face. She gasped at his intent but when he pulled her down and thrust his tongue deep within her, she did not have the strength or the will to protest. He held her still while he made love to her with his mouth. His tongue plundered her repeatedly and then kissed her into oblivion as his lips and tongue laved her clitoris. She clung to the headboard for support as he gave her almost unbearable pleasure. He was as determined as she had been that she allow him to feast on her until she was limp with satisfaction. Even after countless contractions, her hips continued to undulate with delight.

He brought her down to lie in his arms and he kissed her cheeks and lips repeatedly. "You are so wonderful."

"Jade, I have never known anything like this. I didn't know it could feel so good. Last night and every other night we spent together was amazing, but this is lightning and thunder and supernovas. Thank you," she kissed him solemnly as if sealing a promise.

"Nothing in my life has ever prepared me for you. You are magic,' he confessed.

Her heart was content and her body was completely satisfied. They slept the dreamless sleep of the blessed. Only later did she realize there had been no words of love. Would she only hear 'I love you" in her dreams?

☾* ~ Chapter X ~ *☽

The next morning, just before dawn Elizabeth and Evangeline slipped through the woods to Lyle Sessions's house. They had dressed as they had seen it done in the movies, in all black. As they neared the house, they stopped and peered through the underbrush. "What are we looking for?" Evangeline whispered. Maybe, she should have asked that before they left the house.

"Something that I can read, something that he has touched so I can delve into that sick mind of his. I believed he may be responsible for some of those deaths. I'm going to look. I know he's guilty, if he's not guilty of murder - he's certainly guilty of something. The man is as mean as a snake." As Elizabeth studied the white bungalow house, she noticed a clothes line that was strung between the posts on the back porch. A few items of clothing were hanging there secured by clothes pins. "Stay here, I'm going after one of those shirts."

Elizabeth took off, slinking low to the ground. Evangeline didn't have a chance to grab her or stop her, so she prayed that she wouldn't be detected. The early morning light still shone through thick shadows, camouflaging most of her movements. When she reached the porch, she climbed up over the railing until she could reach an old plaid shirt that was flapping in the winter wind. As she leaned over to unhook it from the clothes pins, her eyes focused on something odd. There were hides tacked all over the wall of the house. Cat hides! Domestic cat hides! Lord, she was glad that Evangeline wasn't close enough to see this. She would die! Elizabeth hoped that none of these poor cat skins belonged to any of Arabella's cats that had gone missing over the years. Flashes of howls and yowls of tortured animals flitted through her mind. Residual horror lingered near the skins of these poor babies who had done no wrong other than wander onto a madman's property. Shaking her head to eradicate the stomach-turning images, she turned around and saw the clincher. There was one other hide, a curly white canine hide. Poor Pumpkin. There was no doubt, the son of a bitch was guiltier than hell. Climbing down, she took off in a run. As she hit the ground, the back door opened and out came old Lyle Sessions, a deer rifle in his hand. Elizabeth hit the ground, quickly crawled under the side of the house and clambered to the other side. When she emerged, she ran as fast as she could to the cover of the woods. Looking quickly around she realized that she had missed where Evangeline was standing by a good 100 yards or more.

Out of nowhere, a shot rang out and pieces of bark flew through the air after a bullet from Sessions rifle hit a nearby tree. She fled toward Evangeline, her niece's safety foremost in her mind. Another shot rang out and she zigzagged through the underbrush, desperately scanning the area for the younger girl.

Suddenly, Evangeline grabbed her shirt from the back and together they headed toward *Wildflower Way*. Elizabeth did not look back, but clutched the shirt in one hand and Evangeline's arm in the other – they dashed through the woods, until the Victorian farmhouse came into view.

"Damn thieving, witches – your time is short," he spat at the retreating figures. He didn't know why they wanted a shirt of his, but he knew they were up to no good.

****

Arabella dressed a blue candle with High John the Conqueror Oil. This was strong, hoodoo oil used to empower spells and assert your will. She carved Jade's name into the candle and wrote a petition on a piece of parchment paper.

'Heal Jade Landale from all ills.'

She lit the candle and placed the paper beneath it. Saying a prayer to the gods for his continued healing, she placed the candle next to their bed. 'Their bed', she thought. Just a brief remembrance of his touch sent her head spinning in dangerous directions.

She forced herself to abandon that line of thought. The physical therapist that Dr. Francois had located, was here and working with Jade in the sun room. She had brought a massage table and an exercise bar and some other equipment that she thought would be beneficial to his progress.

As she was straightening the room, and cleaning up from her ritual, a slight knock was heard on the door. She turned to find the physical therapist. "Miss Landry, would you mind if I showed you a massage technique that would help Mr. Landale between my visits?"

"No, I will be right there." She quickly finished and headed to the sun room. She had no experience with massage, she didn't quite know what to expect. She found Jade lying face down on the table with a towel draped over his hips. Her heart missed a beat, he looked so vulnerable. He also looked sexier than any man had a right to look.

The therapist showed her how to place her hands on his back and to work the muscles on either side of his spine. She told her to pay special attention to his lower back and the muscles that covered his taut hips. "It's important that the blood circulates freely through these muscles. If you have any oil, it would be good if you would heat it and use it to lubricate the area. Make sure you rub the oil between your hands to warm it." As the therapist explained the technique, Arabella knew that it would be one of the hardest things that she had ever done. How could she keep her mind on a beneficial massage, when all she wanted to do was make love to him?

The therapist told Jade that he could get off the table, but Jade refrained, "I think I'll lay here for a few moments, if that's okay with you. I'm a little tired." Since the physical therapist would be returning every day or two, the equipment was going to remain.

"Rest as long as you need to. Miss Landry would you show me out?" With a glance back at Jade, to ascertain if he was he in pain; Arabella walked the lady to the door.

Back in the sun room, Jade groaned with arousal. The reason he hadn't gotten up was not pain, but the reaction to the idea of Arabella giving him a massage and warming the oil in her hands. Before he had realized what was happening he had swelled to embarrassing proportions. By the time Arabella reentered the sun room, he was beginning to regain control of his wayward body.

"Jade, are you OK?"

He laughed, "Yes, I just didn't want to embarrass you." He rolled over and carefully sat up, rearranging the towel. Arabella couldn't help but see the blatant evidence of his aroused state. She tried to hide it, but her face fell. Jade had been turned on by the attractive young woman's touch.

"No need to be embarrassed. It's normal. She is a very beautiful young woman and I am sure she gives a very good massage." He was silent for a moment and then he understood.

Catching her hand, he drew her to him. "It wasn't the technician that turned me on, honey, it was the idea of your hands on my body that created this monster." He spread his legs and pulled her between them. Taking her head in both of his hands, he pressed tender kisses all over her face. "It's you that I want; it's you that makes my blood boil and my heart race. Just as soon as I get clearance from Dr. Francois, I am going to show you just what you mean to me."

****

Arabella had promised Jade that she would visit his home and collect some of his things. He had not asked her again, but she didn't want to keep him waiting. After they had ate lunch, Jade had gone to rest and Arabella took out the directions that he had wrote down for her, the list that he had made and the keys that would get her into his house.

The house was actually a loft in downtown Austin. It was right in the midst of the city, very near the huge university, the capitol building and the infamous 6th street entertainment district.

The drive didn't take her but about a half hour. Parking shouldn't be a problem, because Jade had a reserved spot. When she located the spot, however, there was a white Audi parked in the place. She had to drive to another level of the garage and park in the visitors' area. The loft was on the 5th floor of the newly renovated building and she had to use his key card to enter the elevator, and then again, to gain access to the wing where his apartment was housed.

When she found the door of his loft, she slipped the key in and entered. It took her breath away. No expense had been spared; the apartment was decorated and furnished with the very best. ***Wildflower Way*** was comfortable, but there was really no comparison between the two. 'Jade must feel like he's slumming,' she thought. She walked through the living area and found his study. He had wanted his checkbook and some other papers that he had left in his desk. When she started to turn the knob that would let her into the study, she noticed that a light was shining from under the door. Thinking he must have left a light on, she opened the door and was shocked to find Kate Thompson sitting at his desk. Miss Thompson was equally surprised to find herself being interrupted by a stranger.

"Who are you?" She shouted at Arabella. "I'll call the police!" Kate Thompson threatened her.

"I'm Arabella Landry, Miss Thompson. Jade is staying with me. I just came to pick up some of his things."

Arabella could tell that she had pulled the rug out from under the other girl. "Jade is staying with you? What, do you run some type of a private rehabilitation center or something?"

"Or something." was the only answer she gave the stunning woman.

"Where exactly is my fiancé?" The words pierced Arabella to the heart.

"I didn't think the engagement was still on?" Arabella pointed out in a low voice.

"That is none of your business, but the engagement is most certainly still on," she yelled. "I demand to see my fiancé. Give me the address."

"He is at ***Wildflower Way*** in Wimberley." Arabella gave her one of her cards. She didn't want to, but maybe Jade would want to see Kate – after all, they had been engaged. When Kate Thompson stood up, Arabella realized that the outcome of their reunion might be one that broke her heart.

Kate Thompson was so beautiful. She was as tall as Jade and had striking Nordic coloring and a body that was perfect in every way. Arabella knew that next to Kate Thompson, she would come up sadly lacking. "What are you doing here?" The blonde demanded.

"I am picking up some clothes and papers that Jade asked for," she explained politely.

"Well, you just don't need to bother. I will bring them to him and soon I will bring him back here – with me – where he belongs." She stood back and watched the other woman get the checkbook, the papers and then go to his bedroom and take a suitcase out of the closet and then place a few items in it. She didn't have to look for anything; it was obvious that Kate Thompson knew her way around Jade's bedroom like it was her own. As Arabella watched her, she realized that there were women's clothes in the closet and shoes on the floor and in the bathroom there was feminine toiletries ensconced in the vanity and in the cabinet.

Doubt and misgivings ripped into her. Quietly, without letting Kate see her leave, Arabella slipped out. It was obvious that the Nordic beauty was in charge. Without any official status to claim, Arabella backed off and went back to Wimberley to tell Jade that he was about to have company.

****

Arabella drove faster than the law allows to get back to Jade and the rest of her family. When she pulled up in the driveway, she was driving fast enough to throw a little gravel to one side. She headed to the back so she could talk to Elizabeth and the rest before she saw Jade. The possible outcomes of this situation were tearing her up. When she entered the kitchen, it was fully occupied; Nanette was peeling potatoes, Evangeline was making a salad, Elizabeth was icing a cake and Angelique was frying old-fashioned Southern Fried chicken. Her stomach reacted to the aromas that wafted through the room, but she couldn't think about food now.

Everyone looked at her expectantly; it was obvious that she was distraught. "Kate Thompson will be here any minute."

"What?" Evangeline asked, amazed. "I thought she was out of the picture."

"So did I." Arabella admitted.

"She wants him back, now that he is going to recover." Elizabeth read the situation.

"When I went in that apartment, I could tell that he is wealthy. I would say she is after his money, but anyone would want him, even if he was a pauper. Jade is worth a million times whatever money he has." Arabella was shaking. "The picture in the paper, it didn't do her justice. She is statuesque, blond, built, and determined."

"Jade loves you." Nanette spoke lowly but emphatically.

"He hasn't said so." Arabella confessed.

"He doesn't have to," Elizabeth assured her. "His heart calls out to yours. I can hear it, baby." She walked over and hugged her daughter. "Now, get in there and tell your man his EX fiancé is on her way."

They all stayed in the kitchen and out of the way, while she went in search of Jade. She found him doing basic exercises that the physical therapist had shown him how to do. She had left some small weights for him to work out with that would help him regain complete control of his arm and shoulder muscles.

When he saw her, his face broke out in a joyous smile. "Hey, baby. That didn't take long." He looked at her as if to ask where the items were. "Did you get my cell phone?"

"Jade, I didn't get anything." At his confused look, she just said it. "Kate was there when I arrived." She watched the changes on his face carefully. He frowned a bit, but she pressed on. "She wouldn't let me take your things. She is bringing them herself and she will be here any minute."

Right on cue, the front door bell rang. Arabella did not wait to hear what he had to say, she didn't want to see the joy that might travel over his features.

When Arabella opened the door, Kate just marched in, suitcase and travel bag in hand. "Where is he?" Arabella led her to Jade's room. He hadn't moved. In fact, he went right on lifting the weights. The thick, strong muscles in his arms rippled and there was no doubt in either one of the women's mind that this was a real man who, no doubt, would regain complete control of every muscle in his body.

"Oh darling how wonderful to see you." Kate laid down the cases and threw herself at Jade. Jade dropped the weights and held up his hands to stop her forward progress.

"Kate." He said her name simply and shortly.

"Why didn't you call me, sweetheart? What are you doing in this caretaker's home? You can afford to hire someone to work out of our home." She was caressing his hair and face and Arabella felt like she was about to die.

Technically, that was exactly why Jade was here. She was his caretaker. In fact that was the arrangement she had offered to him, that she would bring him back here and take care of him. When she heard this woman say the obvious, it did sound like a simple business arrangement.

"I didn't call you because you made it plain that you wanted nothing to do with me. Did you think that I had forgotten that you left your ring lying on my chest?"

The wheels were turning in Kate Thompson's mind. "I would never have left you had I known that there was any chance that you would get better." Arabella did not understand why Kate thought that terse explanation placed her in any better light.

"Exactly. Kate, I was aware of everything. I could hear every word that anybody said. You could have talked to me and encouraged me. You could have sat with me and comforted me, but you couldn't bear to be in the same room with me."

"I have never been good with sick people, but I'm here now. Just as soon as your doctor says it is safe for you to be moved, we will go home together." At that declaration, Kate swung around to Arabella. "What are you still doing in here? Give me and my fiancé some privacy."

"Don't go anywhere, Arabella." Jade spoke to her

gently. At the change in tone of voice, Kate turned to look at him.

"Why are you talking to the help that way, Jade? She is nothing to you."

"You're wrong, Kate. She is everything to me. *You* are nothing to me."   Kate Thompson's face blanched white. "I'm not going anywhere with you and before you leave – give me my key."

"Jade, no, we love each other."   All of a sudden, Kate Thompson had turned pitiful.   "We're the same kind of people, you and I."

"Give me my key, Kate."

She handed it over.

"My things are still there," she whispered.

"I will have them boxed up and delivered to your parent's door."

"You need me and Daddy, Jade."   Kate whispered, giving it one more shot.

"If that's the only way I can win, I don't want it." His answer clearly and effectively ended the subject. Arabella walked behind Kate as the angry woman stormed out of the room and then out of the door.

When Arabella closed the door behind her, she turned around and Jade had rolled the wheelchair out to where she was. "I'm sorry about that, Bella." He pulled her down to his lap. She tried to get up, so afraid that she would hurt him. "Be still." He held her close.

"Are you sure, Jade? She is so very beautiful."

"Yes, she is beautiful, but she is as cold as ice. I don't know what I was thinking about with her. You, on the other hand are not only beautiful, but also warm and sweet and hot and responsive." He nuzzled her neck and nipped at her ear lobe.

"We haven't made love, yet. I hope I . ." he didn't let her finish.

"Dr. Francois is on his way over and that is the main question that I want answered.   I want you so much, and I feel like I am well enough to love you completely."

"We can wait."

"No, we can't." He was adamant in his desire to consummate their relationship. He rolled them both back into the room and as she moved from his lap, he picked up his travel bag. Looking inside, he drew out his checkbook and other papers. "I want to help with the expenses," he began.

"No, you are my guest." She contradicted him.

"Arabella, I am adding to your bills in every way. I have money and there is no reason for me not to pay for my part and more."

"No, I will help you file your insurance in the case of the doctor and the physical therapist, but I will pay for the household expenses. I enjoy taking care of you." He looked at her carefully, his eyes narrowing. This was new to him; everybody always wanted what he could give them. He was about to approach the argument from a different angle, when Dr. Francois stuck his head through the door.

"How does my miracle patient feel?"

"Stronger every minute." Jade admitted. "Arabella, could you excuse us a moment?" Being dismissed, Arabella retreated to the kitchen. She knew that Jade had some pointed questions for the doctor.

Evangeline was waiting at the door of the dining room, wanting to know what had happened with Kate. Her eyes widened in curiosity. "He sent her on her way." Arabella admitted gratefully. Arabella walked next to her cousin. The kitchen was empty. "Where is everybody?"

"A woman came who wanted a little help getting her boyfriend back. They took her back to your' craft' room and are fixing her a gris-gris bag." Evangeline enjoyed her play on words when referring to the room where Arabella kept all of her witchcraft supplies and where she kept her small altar of special items that she used in ritual – the 'craft' room.

Arabella couldn't be still. Evangeline could tell that she was upset from her run in with Kate Thompson and then the doctor's visit. It was so thrilling to know that Jade had made such a complete turnaround, but Arabella had enough sense to know that he still had a long way to go.

He wasn't able to walk on his own yet and it wasn't clear how long it would be until he could."

The door to the bedroom opened and Dr. Francois called her back in. She returned, her eyes anxiously meeting Jade's to see if she could read his mood. She couldn't.

"Sit down, Miss Landry."

She obeyed. "Jade is actually improving faster than is beyond my understanding. The muscle reflexes are better today than they were, even yesterday. I would ask you to give him massage therapy tonight and he is understandably anxious to resume sexual activity," Arabella felt her face flush with embarrassment. He continued, "and I have given my permission, if you will be content to be the one on top, so as not to put extra pressure on his back."

Arabella thought she would die. This type of sexual frankness was beyond her comprehension. "I would never want Jade to take any undue chances."

Dr. Francois was clinical and did not appear to be uncomfortable with the conversation at all. When she glanced at Jade, his eyes were smoldering with such heat that she felt her clothing might catch fire. As she walked the doctor to the door, her mother met her in the corridor. "Sweetie, Tyler called and he wants to take us all out to dinner. How about it?" Unique opportunity, Arabella thought.

As soon as she thought it, Elizabeth picked up on the train of thought. "Okay, sweetie. You stay here and make love to your man and I'll have a good time with everybody else."

"Thanks, Mom." This time she didn't protest at her mother's mind reading.

****

They had the house to themselves. She prepared them a simple supper and went about taking care of a few mundane activities. He did the same; he was becoming more independent by the hour. The doctor had insisted that she continue with his massage therapy and the idea of having unbridled access to his body sent chills through her soul. They would have to go into the sun room for that part of the evening. She hoped that she could keep her head about her and not attack him out here in the sun room. After she finished what she needed to do and completed her bath; she washed and dried her hair.

Descending the stairs, she checked to make sure all the doors and windows were locked per her grandmother's request. She left the deadbolt off of the front door so the gang could get back in when they returned from their outing. When she went to the sunroom she was surprised to find that the massage table had been moved. She wondered if Jade had got somebody to move it for him or had he foolishly moved it alone? She hoped he had not hurt himself. Then the thought of his explanation to anyone who might have helped him – 'would you please help me move the massage table to my room so Arabella and I can . . . . . ." Her thoughts wouldn't go that far.

Regardless of how it was done, she secretly thrilled to the prospect of her hands on his body. She was wearing a snow white eyelet ensemble and her hair hung straight and thick, a startling contrast to the color of her robe. She found him waiting on her; he was sitting on the side of the bed, unabashedly nude.

He stared at her with hot smoldering eyes. "I've been waiting for you."

She did not know what to say, so she said nothing. "Are you ready for your massage?" She tried to be professional about it; straightening the soft mattress and the coverlet so that he could lie down in comfort. She averted her glance while he stood and eased himself up on the table. She was aware that he did not attempt to cover himself and she was well aware that only last night she had loved every inch of his substantial manhood – right now she was as shy as she had ever been in her life. The table protested his weight and when all sound of his settling himself down ceased, she turned to look at him on the table. Her breath caught. His broad, tan back completely covered the surface, making the table seem almost miniature. His backside was begging to be touched – one hand was tempted to brush his hip – but she jerked it back realizing that real work had to be done. She came near to him, trying to remember what the physical therapist had told her. The bottle of oil was sitting on the bedside table and she poured some in one palm and then rubbed her hands together, warming the oil. She took a deep breath and began: working the muscles of his back, rubbing out the knots and kneading the hard, warm flesh. Arabella visualized healing blue light coming from her fingertips, using this opportunity to ply her traiteur skills. She moved her hands up his back and then down, paying careful attention to his spine. She drew her hands down both sides and then settled on his lower back intensifying the pressure that she was putting on his muscles. Despite the wisdom of the act, she could not resist massaging his beautiful buttocks. She heard him groan at her fevered touch.

"Arabella, I'm coming off this table, before I come on this table." Even though the remark was meant to be humorous, she did not feel like laughing.

She felt like losing her virginity.

She stepped back as he dismounted the table. His penis was already completely distended, full and heavy with need. "You look like a virgin bride in this gown," he whispered. She swallowed hard and answered him carefully.

"I am a virgin." What she wasn't saying, was how she longed to be his bride.

"Not for long." He pulled the robe off of her shoulders and the gown over her head.

"I don't think we finished your massage."

"You can touch me anytime you want to, sweetheart, but right now I am dying to touch you – all over." He drew her down into the bed and then he covered her with his body.

"Be careful with your back," she warned.

"Don't worry, I plan on following the doctor's instructions, but right now I feel wonderful."

She hugged his neck and kissed his eyes and cheeks, "I am so glad that you feel better. I want you to walk and run and do everything that you used to do, and everything that you ever wanted to do." Her lips moved across his jaw and down his neck, her tongue darting out to taste his salty skin. Jade endured her tiny kisses until they became unbearable. He pulled her arms from around his neck and pulled them over her head preventing her from moving an inch. She was completely at his mercy.

"Remember how you teased me, ordered me not to move, tormented me with your hands and mouth?"

"Yes." She gasped hoarsely.

"It's my turn, now," he breathed. And so it began. He kissed her face, her lips, and her neck: warm, gentle kisses that spoke words to her heart that his lips had not uttered. He lowered himself in the bed, until his face was even with her full, round breasts. He put a hand on either side of her breasts and he pushed them together. His gaze scorched her skin. He rubbed his face over the soft mounds of flesh, and then he began feasting on them with his mouth. He paid special attention to the nipples, he knew she loved having her nipples kissed and suckled. As he paid homage to her breasts, taking as much of them into his mouth as possible, she began to moan.

She had promised to be still, but he felt the little movements began. Despite her best efforts to be motionless, her hips began to undulate in small tight circles. Still he licked, nibbled, kissed and massaged his breasts with his tongue and lips. Her nipples were swollen and hard. At his attention her breasts swelled and grew proud with the love that was being lavished on them. Finally, he moved lower, kissing down her narrow waist and over her flaring hips. He pressed his lips on the very edge of her womanhood. She was so tense, her hips beginning to lift slightly, offering herself to him in soundless surrender. "Climb on top of me now, Bella." He lay down and pulled himself back on the pillows so his head would be elevated.

She did as she was told. Unaware of her actions, she touched her own breasts pulling slightly at the nipples. He couldn't take his eyes off of her. She straddled his hips, waiting for him to give her further leeway to the treasures to come. "Raise up on your knees, sweetheart." She did so and he cupped her vagina, massaging the labia and inserting his fingers deep inside her. He was thrilled to find that she was hot and wet and more than ready for him. Still, it was her first time and he would have died before he ever caused her any pain or discomfort. He continued to move his hand rhythmically inside of her, she began to tremble slightly.

"Jade, please, please put him inside of me." He smiled at the 'him'. She was the sweetest thing. She was so responsive, even while he was in the throes of passion he could not help but compare her and Kate – and Kate came up way short. At her request, he took his own member in his hand and gently guided the head of it to brush against her canal. In their dreams, this had been thrilling, but now it was ten thousand times better, because she was here in his arms and he was free to move and shout and buck and pleasure this woman to his heart's content. His penis was in position and he could feel her heat welcome his arrival. "Now, baby began to lower yourself down and take as much of my shaft as you can stand. If it starts to hurt, I'll pull out. You're in control now."

Arabella took a deep breath and began to lower herself on his huge sex. Initially, her muscles rebelled at the invasion but gradually they grew accustomed to the new sensations and they began to relax and accommodate his throbbing rod. Joy began to bubble up inside of her. She was doing it! She was stretching, easing down and accommodating more and more of him, until at last her hips settled on his groin and she was filled completely. She felt a sense of power and an uncontrollable desire to move. He lifted up his hands and she weaved her fingers into his, using them to balance and support, as she began to rotate her hips in small circles. He caught his breath and closed his eyes. Then, she began to slowly rock back and forth, still rotating her hips. She marveled at the pleasure each movement brought. Arabella grew bolder, lifting herself, until she was stroking his shaft from the top to the bottom with her sheath, the interior muscles contracting, grasping and squeezing. She brought his hands to her breasts, offering them as a sacrifice to his roughened fingertips and hungry palms. Over and over again, she slid up and down the thick pole, making sure he was loved to the full measure. Even though this was her first time, his desire, his pleasure and his need was never out of her mind. He threw his head back and the muscles in his neck corded with tension, he began to raise his hips as the heat began to build. A volcanic eruption was imminent.

Arabella was amazed. The pleasure, the friction was so perfect that she felt that this was what she had been born for – to accept and treasure each stroke and caress. His hands on her nipples pushed her over the edge – she lost herself – slamming down against him repeatedly. The velvet caress of her impossibly tight sheath catapulted him into oblivion. He exploded inside her, shooting his come deep within her womb. The pleasure was relentless as she massaged, convulsed, and clenched him in maddening, white-hot lava. Even after he was spent, her interior muscles kept involuntarily contracting around him, tenderly insuring that he felt every ounce of ecstasy that was his to claim. At the very end, she ground her hips into his, allowing the pearl of her clitoris to spasm against the ridge of his pelvic bone.

Still cherishing him deep within her, she leaned down on him surrendering to his gentle embrace. He marveled at her natural, inborn passion. None of his past experiences had ever prepared him for this temptress. She had no idea how precious she was. His voice caught in his throat when he tried to speak. "Bella, I have no words. It was perfect. You are perfect." They slept still joined in the most intimate of ways.

☾* ~ Chapter XI ~ *☽

The time with Detective Garrison had meant more to Elizabeth than she would ever admit. She could tell that he was interested in her. Her feelings weren't so easy to define. Despite her brashness, Elizabeth felt things very deeply. After Tom, she had sworn to never let her heart become so bound to another person. Her husband's death had been a near fatal blow to her heart. Now, she was torn between the possibility of a new beginning and the safe haven of her life as it was now.

The time had arrived, however, to read Lyle Sessions garment. She held it in her hands, the closeness of something that had touched his body made her skin crawl. Despite her revulsion, she ran her fingers over the fibers. Then the blinding visions came. She saw Kathy and Lea cowering on the ground at Lyle Sessions' feet. The crazed man, heaving with excitement, drew back a weapon and began to club Kathy Townsend over the head. Their terrified screams pierced Elizabeth's heart. After three or four blows, Kathy quit screaming. The little girl was crying 'Mommy, Mommy, Mommy' over and over again. The last glimpse of horror that Elizabeth gleaned from the killer's shirt was one final blow to the little girl's skull. At that time, she saw the weapon was undeniably, a large baseball bat drenched in blood.

****

Elizabeth shuddered with the confirmation that Lyle Sessions killed their neighbors. Cold chills ran down her back as she remembered Evangeline's encounter in the woods and the close proximity that both of them had been to the psycho just yesterday. She dialed Tyler on her cell and he answered after two rings.

"Detective Garrison."

"Tyler, its Elizabeth."

"Hey, it's good to hear your voice. Last night was fun,

but next time I'd like for it to be just us."

"I think that can be arranged." Elizabeth said. Tyler could tell that she wasn't her usual bantering self.

"What's wrong Elizabeth?"

"I told you last night that I took one of Session's shirts from the clothes line in order to see if I could get any psychic information from it."

Tyler let out a long breath. "Yes, I've been expecting him to come in and file a complaint on you all morning."

"He won't do that." She replied emphatically.

"Why not, did you put a spell on him?" He teased.

"No, he's guilty of murder and he won't risk getting that close to you or any police officer."

"What did you see, Elizabeth?"

"I saw Sessions club Kathy and Lea to death with a wooden boat paddle."

"Elizabeth, as much as I would like to go over and search every inch of Sessions property, I can't get a warrant based on a vision. I need more." She could tell by his voice that he wanted to act on her revelation, but his hands were tied. She understood.

"Well, he's insane. He tortures animal, I found dozens of cat hides nailed to his house and shed. So, I trust that he will slip up and give you some concrete reason to search his property. I just hope that no one else has to die before that happens." Tyler could tell that Elizabeth was disappointed, and it hurt his heart to let her down.

****

Arabella received an early morning phone call from Rachel Townsend. The bodies of her family had finally been released by the coroner and she was making funeral arrangements. Arabella's heart bled for her.

"Let me help you, Rachel."

"I don't even know what to ask for." Rachel confessed.

"Let us bring food over for your visiting relatives, and please, let us come over and give your house a good cleaning for you. I know you don't feel like doing that and it would mean a lot to me to be able to do something for you."

This touched Rachel and she agreed to bring a key over for Arabella. She was staying at her sister's house in San Antonio. The house just had too many memories for her to be able to endure staying there by herself, just yet. Kathy's ex-husband and other relatives would be coming in for the wake and the funeral, so the Wimberley house was the logical place for them to stay.

After completing the call, Arabella went to check on Jade. He was with the physical therapist and Arabella was overjoyed to find she had him up and walking. Arabella caught her breath watching him attempt to cross the sun room. When the young woman had arrived, Arabella had been embarrassed helping her move the massage table back to where it would be used. Her name was Lisa, and gratefully, she had not asked any questions.

Jade was making wonderful progress. Arabella could not imagine him even needing a cane in a matter of weeks. The nerves and muscles were responding well and each step he took seemed to be easier than the last. Dr. Francois had insisted that Jade make an appointment at the hospital, so a full brain scan could be taken and he could properly evaluate the area that had been so severely injured in the fall.

In a short while, Jade would be well enough to do anything he wanted to. Arabella trusted him implicitly, but she could not help but wonder where she would fit into his life once he regained his complete health. He had an important and promising career to return to and his attention would be pulled in many different directions. She hoped that the gods would give her strength to realize that she would have to share him with many other people.

Leaving them alone to complete his therapy, Arabella began to gather supplies to take to the Townsend house to ready it for its sad task.

Evangeline found Arabella in the kitchen where she was filling a box with floor cleaner, furniture polish and other supplies. "What are you doing?"

"I am about to go to the Townsend's and clean the house in preparation for Kathy and Lea's funeral."

"Oh, no – we were all about to drive in to Austin for lunch and I have an appointment with one of the orientation advisers to get a private tour of the campus. Let me try and reschedule so we can go and help you." Arabella could tell that Evangeline was certainly willing to change her plans, but she knew that this was something that her cousin had been looking forward to for years.

"Absolutely not. I am perfectly capable of cleaning a house on my own. I'll scoot over there and take care of this and be back by the time you are."

"Are you sure?" Evangeline never liked to disappoint her cousin.

Arabella gave Evangeline a quick hug and kiss. "Have a good time."

****

From the time that she and Jade had got up this morning, the activity in the household had been so persistent that they had not had a chance to have a moment alone. She had slipped out of bed while he was still asleep to get some orders in the mail. Her intentions had been to return to bed and wake him with a tender kiss, but the physical therapist had called and said she needed to move his appointment up from ten a.m. to eight a.m.

Now, Arabella needed to go to the Townsend's and fulfill her promise before people began arriving from out of town. She looked for Jade to tell him her plans. She wished that he could go with her, but she didn't know if his wheelchair would fit into her car. She headed toward the sunroom and found a smiling Jade standing up and walking slowly with the help of an aluminum cane. If she hadn't been afraid of hurting him, she would have thrown herself at him in sheer joy. "Look at you!" She gasped.

"Lisa said I am making excellent progress." He was obviously pleased with himself.

"I am so proud of you."

"You alone are responsible for this, Arabella." He grew serious. "You came to me when I needed you most and you didn't give up until you rescued me from total despair and worse."

The words he said were beautiful, but Arabella was suddenly chilled listening to them. She didn't want his gratitude, she wanted his love. She would accept any affection that he offered, but she swore in her heart that she would never make any demands on him. He must never feel that he owed her anything. Mentally, she shook her head – now was not the time to dwell on her own feelings. The important thing was Jade and his recovery. Putting a smile on her face, she answered him. "I am just thankful that I found you."

He noticed the box of cleaning supplies on the floor next to her. "What are you doing?"

"I have to go to Rachel Townsend's. I promised her that I would give her house a quick cleaning. The funeral arrangements have been made for Kathy and Lea, the relatives will all be coming in and Rachel is in no shape to handle this alone. Tomorrow we will take food over so they won't have to worry about cooking."

"That's so considerate of you. Can I come along?"

"Of course," she readily agreed. "Now that you're mobile, you are free to do anything your heart desires."

His eyes immediately darkened with passion. "What I want to do is take you back to bed; but I'll settle for watching you clean."

Her cheeks flushed, if they were together for seventy years, he would always have the power to bring instant heat to her body. "I will always want you with me. However, you don't have to go over there. You can stay here and catch up on the news or read, if you'd rather. I am used to being by myself."

"You have me now. You don't ever have to be alone again."

Words like that could not go unrewarded. For just a moment, she carefully enfolded him in her arms and pressed a chaste kiss on his cheek. His promise warmed her heart, she prayed that he would always feel that way, but she vowed that she would never tie him down. When he got strong enough and ready to go back to his world, she would try her best to be glad for him.

****

There were eyes in the woods. Evil was keeping a constant vigil of the comings and goings at *Wildflower Way*.

The trip to the Townsend home was not ignored.

****

She had helped him into the car, loaded the cleaning supplies and quickly made the short trip to Rachel's home. Arabella held her breath as he carefully maneuvered the steps into the house. She didn't want to be a nuisance, but she had sense enough to know that a fall could be devastating. The medical tests were scheduled for the following morning and she couldn't wait to hear the results. Perhaps, the news would alleviate much of her worry.

The kitchen and downstairs living area was where she wanted to begin, so she helped Jade find a comfortable place where he could see her for most of the time. She turned on Rachel's television and bent over him for a quick kiss before she began her work. The kiss turned into more than she had originally planned, for he seized the moment and laid claim to her lips. It was so tempting to sink down into the chair with him and indulge herself in his arms, but she playfully pushed him away, "Time for that later, Romeo. I have work to do."

He reluctantly let her go and she began her chores. Arabella had never minded cleaning, so she found her rhythm and made good progress.

****

After Elizabeth's disturbing report to Detective Garrison, he had decided to go the extra mile for her. Even if he could not legally search Sessions property, he could put *Wildflower Way* and the Sessions home under surveillance.

The officer that drew that duty was Officer Kyle Myers. He was a local boy who knew all of the parties involved and wasn't surprised to find that Lyle Sessions could somehow be a player. He was totally skeptical about all that psychic business, but he couldn't explain everything else that had happened, either.

He had stationed himself across the road from the herb farm and when the couple had left, he had discreetly followed them to the Townsend home. Now, he was parked so he could see both the Sessions place and the scene of the crimes. All he had to do now was just wait and see if anything happened.

****

Finishing the downstairs, she thought about informing Jade that she was heading upstairs to change linens and clean the bathrooms. Her mood had significantly lightened and she was looking forward to finishing here and taking Jade home where they could, hopefully, spend some time alone together before the rest of the family got back from Austin.

As she stepped into the room, her world crashed around her feet – she couldn't utter a single word.

Lyle Sessions was standing at one end of the room with a deer rifle pointed at Jade's head. "You whore witch, I am sick and tired of your meddling, fiendish ways. It's time that you paid for your sins. I'm gonna to kill your lover and then I'm gonna to kill you."

Jade did not blink. He was frozen; there was no chance that he could get out of the way. He had managed to beat death one time, and here he was again staring it right in the face. He looked at Arabella, who was as white as a sheet; at least she had a chance to get out of this alive. "Run, Bella, run," he commanded her.

Arabella heard his voice and decided to obey, although not in the way that he had meant. Allowing this maniac to kill her love was completely out of the question. Instantly, she measured the distance that she would have to cover and obeyed his voice without hesitation. With a prayer to the gods for strength, speed and safety, she ran. She moved heaven and earth as she covered the endless distance between the point where she had stood in horror, to the place where the shot was passing from Sessions rifle to connect with Jade's body.

Arabella Landry intercepted the bullet that was meant for Jade Landale.

The bullet caught her in the upper back and passed brutally through her body, leaving a large exit wound in the front, over her left breast. The force of the blast threw her at Jade's feet. She gasped from the red-hot rending pain and then she knew no more.

Horrified, Jade watched her fall, a seeming fountain of blood seeping into the front of her white sweater, turning it from snow to crimson.

Time stood still for Jade and Arabella.

Jade instantly fell to his knees and desperately sought to stop the flow of blood with his bare hands, he seemed totally unaware that the killer was still in the room with him.

Lyle Sessions, however, was not through. Although he had not hit the one he was aiming at, he had shot the witch. One down, one to go.

Unbeknownst to either Jade or the killer, Officer Myers had quietly slipped around the house and through the kitchen door. As the old man raised the gun to shoot Jade, the young officer burst into the room and another shot rang out. Sessions grabbed his arm and quickly stepped backwards from the room, firing shot after shot at the unnerved police officer. Officer Myers pursued him, but Sessions managed to exit the house and escape into the woods. Kyle Myers had seen Sessions enter the Townsend home. He had known he was up to no good, but as fast as Myers had moved, he had not been fast enough to save Arabella.

The young officer had only minimal experience in dealing with gunshot wounds. He had never seen so much blood. The Congressman was doing his best to stop the bleeding, but it was obvious he needed something to hold over the wounds.

Jade screamed at Myers to get some towels from the kitchen. Myers brought the towels and together they worked frantically to apply enough pressure to the double wound to keep her heart from pumping every bit of her life giving blood from her body. True to his training, the first thing that Myers had done was call for assistance, but he was unsure whether the help would come in time. Sadly, Myers thought that Arabella had as much chance of surviving this attack as an ice cube could survive a Texas heat wave.

The ambulance arrived in record time, but for Jade it seemed an eternity. Tyler Garrison arrived moments after the EMS began working on Arabella. They had been the same team that had transported Jade from ***Tranquility*** to ***Wildflower Way***. Working feverishly, they finally managed to stop the biggest part of the blood flow. Detective Garrison phoned Elizabeth who was already on her way to the hospital.

Adrenaline was pumping through Jade like a flood, he left his cane behind and walked next to the stretcher that held the pale, near lifeless form of the woman; who may very well have given her life to save his. Never had he felt such anguish and humility. There had been love in his childhood, but he had never known that this kind of selfless, sacrifice even existed. She could have run away. She could have saved herself, but she didn't. Jade felt as if his heart had been torn out of his chest.

The EMS attendants loaded Arabella into the back of the ambulance. "You can ride with her if you want," one of them offered. He climbed in, desperately wanting to be wherever she was. One of the men got into the cab to drive, while the other stayed at Arabella's side. Jade was quaking with fear. "Is she going to be all right?" He asked the man whose shirt read 'Robert'.

Robert looked at the ashen, shaken man. He started to lie to him, but it just wasn't his style. "It's going to be touch and go. She's lost an awful lot of blood and her pulse is thready and weak." As if in response to the words, the attached monitor began to beep loudly. "She's coding," the man spoke loudly. The driver, whose siren was already sounding, sped up even faster. Robert took out some paddles and turned on the battery powered unit and he began to shock Arabella's heart, desperately trying to get it started again.

****

As if in a dream, Arabella left her body. She rose above her still form and saw Jade crying at her side. The sensation of floating and freedom was quite pleasant. This experience was not as substantial as their meetings on E-Rock had been. She tried to comfort Jade, but he could not see or hear her. His grief disturbed Arabella. She looked down at herself. Was she dead?

Robert did not give up; he started CPR and then tried the paddles one more time.

"Please come back Arabella," Jade cried. "Please come back, I love you Arabella." Heeding the voice of the one that she loved more than anything else in the world, she submitted to the gravitational pull of her body beckoning her soul to return. The pain was horrid and mind-numbing and if she would have had the strength, she would have cried.

****

"She's back, but I can't promise for how long." The ambulance pulled up into the emergency room entrance. Nurses rushed out to aid the attendants. Jade had to step back and let them wheel her into the emergency room. Elizabeth, Evangeline, Angelique and Nanette all rushed up to him with stricken, tear-streaked faces. "Tell us everything," Nanette demanded.

Jade tried hard to be strong for them as well as for Arabella. "She was working in the kitchen area and I was in the living room. I heard someone come into the room and I looked up thinking it was her. It wasn't, it was an old man. The police officer who shot at him said that it was your neighbor, Lyle Sessions." None of the women looked surprised, only sorrowful. "He called Arabella names and said that he was going to shoot me, then her. He pointed the rifle at me and I froze, I knew there was no way that I could get up and get out of the way. I screamed at Arabella to run," his voice broke, "and she did, but not the right way – Instead of saving herself she ran between us and took the bullet that was meant for me." Tears were spilling from his eyes. "It was all my fault."

Much to his surprise, Nanette denied this. "Even if you

were still in that hospital bed in **Tranquility**, this man would have tried to kill Arabella. We uncovered his crime and he means for us to pay."

Elizabeth agreed with her mother, "There's another thing, Jade. Arabella would do anything in the world to protect you. She loves you a thousand times more than she loves herself. I wished a million times that I could have saved Tom. I would have given everything I had, including my life, for just one more day with him. Count yourself fortunate; not that you are alive, but that you have been loved so completely and so well."

Angelique and Evangeline stepped on either side of Jade and led him into the waiting room. He decided not to hide the rest of the story. "They resuscitated her in the ambulance, her heart stopped and they had to shock her to get it started again. Robert, one of the EMS guys said that she had lost so much blood that he didn't know if she would make it or not."

"She will make it." Nanette said evenly. "I am here and I am willing her to live. I should have thought this through. I put a ward around the house, but then I let her leave the safety of the spell. I bet she forgot and took her gris-gris bag off – if it's anybody's fault, Jade, it's mine. I should have watched after her better."

They sat quietly and waited for what seemed an eternity. At long last, a doctor came into the room and said two words that set them all free. "She's resting."

****

It hurt so badly. The pain was almost unbearable. Arabella fought to open her eyes. She had no strength. Over and over again she tried to remember what had happened. Was Jade OK? She remembered seeing Lyle Sessions and the maniacal sneer on his ugly face. He had been about to kill her Jade. Did she save him? The drugs began to take effect and her grip on reality faded away again.

****

Jade sat by Arabella's bed for eighteen hours. She had endured two surgeries and they had lost her twice, including the time in the ambulance. Four pints of blood had been pumped into her veins. Elizabeth had tried to get him to go home, but he refused. Dr. Francois had come by and urged him to at least let him perform the scheduled tests, but he had refused. Evangeline and Angelique had brought him food and even Nanette had begged him to get some rest, but he refused.

Television crews had come by wanting to interview him, but he had adamantly refused to take any questions right now. When the police report had reached the ears of the media and they had discovered that another incident had taken place at the scene of the previous murder and that one of the same psychics were involved, as well as the sexy Congressman – the airways and newspapers had gone crazy. Reese Phillips had come to try and talk Jade into distancing himself from the situation and to help him come up with some favorable spin to put on the story. Jade had talked to Reese politely, but refused to leave Arabella's side or step away from her – not even for a moment.

He did consent to meet with Reese after Arabella could go home from the hospital, but not before. He was worried to death. Why wouldn't she wake up? The doctor had said that this was her body's way of dealing with the extreme stress that it had been under, but he was frantic with worry.

Since he had left the place where Arabella had been shot, he had not used his cane at all. He hadn't needed it. Frankly, he couldn't spare the time to think about himself, all he could think about was Arabella.

****

Detective Tyler Garrison now had a legitimate suspect in the murder of Kathy and Lea, and possibly the other victims, if the remains and identities checked out with the information that Mrs. Fontenot had given him. Finally the Detective had way more than enough cause to search Sessions home and property. He had sent his men to arrest him for the attempted murder of Arabella Landry, but his house was completely deserted.

Detective Garrison didn't have to wait long before one of his men phoned to say they had found the baseball bat that he had used to kill the McClemore mother and child. That wasn't all that they found. The men had been horrified to find a full fledged torture chamber in Session's basement. There were whips and chains, electrical paddles, all types of surgical knives and even formaldehyde that he could use to subdue and control his victims. One man lost his lunch when they found dozens of rotting cats and dogs that appeared to have been abused and tortured With evidence like this, they should soon be able to spring the trap.

Garrison had tried to protect Arabella and the rest of them, but Sessions had gotten to them anyway. What plagued his mind now was, would they find the other victims – and could they tie Sessions to those murders, as well. On top of that, Sessions was still on the loose, which meant that Elizabeth and her family were still in danger.

****

He parked his pickup truck on the dirt road that led down to Cypress Creek. Stealthily, walking through the thick underbrush, he got as close to the edge of the creek as he dared, so that he could see across the body of water and watch the activity that was taking place within the yellow-taped parcel of land. He counted eight officers, all armed with shovels or black bags. When he saw the blood hounds, he began to back away. One of them raised its huge head and took a deep breath of air, looking over the creek to where he was hiding.

It was time to leave. His handiwork had been discovered. For five years, he had planted his victims in this place where his torment had started. How long would it be before they realized that all the women looked like pale copies of an original painting?

****

Arabella opened her eyes. Where was she? She seemed to be in a hospital room, for a moment she was terrified she was still sitting beside Jade's bed at **Tranquility** and everything that had happened had all been a dream. But, then she realized that it was she that was in the hospital bed. She closed her eyes for a moment trying to remember, and then it all came rushing back to her. Lyle Sessions had found them at the Townsend's home and he had tried to kill Jade.

In panic, she tried to rise up and a wrenching pain caused her to abandon that effort. Where was Jade? Was he all right? Had he been shot? She was hooked up to a pole and there were tubes everywhere and a needle was in her arm. She could see no one in front of her. She looked toward the door and saw no one. She tried to turn toward the window – and then she saw him.

Jade was sitting at her side in a chair. He was bent over with his head in his hands. He looked so tired, but at least he appeared to be healthy. "Jade," she said hoarsely.

He sprang to his feet. "Arabella, O Arabella – Thank God!!!" Jade knelt by her side and placed his head on her hand.

"Jade, are you all right?" As usual, Arabella was more concerned about Jade than she was about herself.

"I am fine." Jade kissed her hand over and over again. "You saved me again. That bullet was meant for me, but you stepped in front of the gun. What am I going to do with you?"

"I don't know." She murmured tiredly – trying to smile – wishing, needing for him to smile. It broke her heart to see worry on his face. "If you had been injured in any way, I would never have been able to forgive myself. This is nothing. I was only worried about you."

He looked at her pale face. About to protest further, she raised the hand that was unbound by tubes and needles and she pressed it to his lips. "No more." He kissed the finger that pressed against his mouth. "Now, tell me; is everyone else all right? Did Sessions get away?"

"The family is fine, but, yes, Sessions escaped. Though your mother did tell me this morning that Detective Garrison has found the murder weapon that killed your neighbors and now they are searching for him officially as the killer. Officer Myers came to our rescue – or rather my rescue – but he didn't succeed in stopping Sessions."

Arabella was too tired to think about all of that. She

wanted nothing more but to go home and lie in Jade's arms. "When can I go home?"

"I don't know. You . .. you've had a pretty bad time of it. You lost a lot of blood and had to be operated on. Arabella, I almost lost you." She raised her hand and wiped the tears from his beautiful face.

"Stop. I'll be fine. I can't stand to see you cry." Arabella's voice broke. He leaned over and kissed her tenderly on the lips and she met his kiss with her own.

She suddenly realized that he was standing, kneeling, leaning everything without benefit of a cane. "You are better?" she asked incredulously.

"I left the cane at the scene of your injury. I was so worried about you that I never gave myself a thought." They held each other, both of them thankful for the well being of the most important person in their life.

****

Nanette, Elizabeth, Evangeline and Angelique along with Tyler Garrison attended the funeral services of Kathy and Lea Townsend. The service was sad, as the funerals of young people invariably are. Rachel was feeble and frail. Kathy's ex-husband was there and he displayed as much self-control as a young father could. Elizabeth knew that if it had been she or Tom standing over their child's coffin, that they wouldn't have been strong either.

****

Arabella was gaining her strength every day. The doctor had said that he saw no reason why she could not complete her convalescence at home. Jade was ecstatic. He had not left her side, but for very short trips to bathe and change or to grab a bite to eat. He slept in a hard, reclining chair that sat by her bed and he held her hand most of the time. The nurses had let her get up and walk and really – for what she had been through – Arabella felt pretty good.

Her mother had been by and reported on the funeral and all of the media attention that the case was receiving. "I don't know what all the fall out is going to be over this fiasco, but your business has certainly picked up." Arabella knew that her mother was teasing her, but she did long to get back to normal and take care of her herbs, her cats, but most especially her family, which certainly included Jade.

☾* ~ Chapter XII ~ *☽

Finally, the day arrived for Arabella to be released. She had been given the green light by the doctor to resume her normal routine - using common sense, of course. The drive from the hospital to *Wildflower Way* had seemed to take forever, but at last she was home. Jade carefully helped Arabella out of the car. He handled her as if she were made of the finest china. She kept insisting that she wouldn't break, but he was not taking any chances.

The whole contingency met in the living room to welcome her home. Angelique had cooked a honey-baked, spiral ham; black eyed peas and cabbage, because Arabella had missed her normal New Year's Day fare while in the hospital. Evangeline had kept up with her orders and Elizabeth and Nanette were busy trying to devise a ritual that would end this horror with their dangerous neighbor.

She made them all happy by eating a decent amount of food, but they soon realized that she needed rest and time alone with Jade more than she needed anything else.

He led her to their bedroom (it was the way they both thought of it now) and gently helped her into the bathroom so that she could freshen herself after days in the clinical atmosphere of medicine and sterile smells. She would not let him help her in her bathroom regime; Arabella wanted to see for herself exactly how the gunshot wounds and the subsequent surgery had scarred her body.

For the first time in their relationship, Arabella locked the bathroom door. Jade had brought her favorite white eyelet set to wear home. She had wanted him to bring just regular clothes, but he had insisted that the bedroom would be her domain for a few more days and he thought that this manner of dress would be more likely to keep her there. Men!

Slowly, she undid the dozens of tiny shell buttons that ran down the front of the gown. It was faster to pull it over her head, but she wasn't sure that she could stand to lift her arms over her head – the pain was still there, if she moved in a certain way. She slid the gown off of her shoulders and stood there completely in the nude. Slowly she raised her head and opened her eyes and what she saw made her shudder.

The damage from the gunshot wound and the subsequent surgery had left a large, raised, angry scar that stood out in marked contrast to the rest of her smooth skin. There was even a tendril of the scar that snaked down over the top of her left breast. She ran a finger over the scar. There was very little pain in the fast healing wound, the real pain was in her heart as she imagined Jade's thoughts as he saw the scars for the first time.

Steeling herself for the full impact, she turned sideways until she could see the matching scar that hailed the entrance wound as the bullet had torn through her flesh. Arabella realized that she should be eternally grateful; Jade was alive and she suffered no real lasting damage. The bullet had missed her heart and her spine. Actually, the blood loss had been the most life threatening aspect of her whole ordeal.

At the final consultation that she had with the doctor, he had told her that the scars would fade with time or if she so desired, plastic surgery could minimize the blemishes. Her mind could digest how lucky and blessed she was – but her heart mourned the ugliness that she could see in the mirror. Jade tapped on the door, "Are you all right, baby?"

She frantically wiped the foolish tears from her eyes and answered, "I'll be right out." She put the gown back on and laboriously closed every button. All she could think about was what was going to happen when she left the bathroom.

Bravely, she opened the door and what she saw made her want to cry all the more. He had lit dozens of candles. They literally bathed the room in their romantic light. The bed had been covered in red rose petals and the covers were turned back invitingly. An ice bucket set on the bedside table with a bottle of champagne chilling and two tall crystal glasses stood ready to be filled.

He stood next to the bed. She stopped for a moment and just looked at him. He was tall, broad, perfectly muscled – skin of burnished gold. He held out his hand to her and she hesitated – this man deserved the very best and he certainly deserved honesty from her.

She wanted him desperately, but what she wanted most of all was for him to be happy. Jade deserved perfection and she knew in her heart that she had not met that requirement prior to the attack; now she wasn't even in the ball park.

She took his hand. He pulled her to him and he held her close. She rested her head on his hard chest and listened to the strong beat of his heart. "Thank you for the beautiful homecoming: the candles, and the rose petals, the champagne."

"I would try to give you the world, if you asked," he whispered as his lips began kissing her neck. His hands went to the top of her robe, to push it off. She knew that now was the time – she had to stop him.

"Wait, I need to show you something first." He allowed her to step back out of his arms. She took his hand and led him back to the bathroom. She turned on both the overhead lights and the much brighter lights that were over the vanity mirror. She wanted him to see the ugly reality without any hiding or pretense.

"Arabella darling, what are we doing?" He asked patiently.

"Before we make love, I want you to see the full impact of the scars in the harsh light of day, so to speak."

"Arabella. . . . . . ."

"No, I want you to see them now, and know that you have a choice." She felt him stiffen at her side. She did not allow herself to try and imagine what he was thinking, she couldn't stand it.

She began undoing the small shell buttons one more time. "The doctor said that they would fade or I could get plastic surgery to reduce the size and the ugly red color. But, I wanted you to see them up front, before we went to bed. I couldn't bear waiting until we were in the throes of passion and then watching your face change when you uncovered the scars."

He stood in front of her; she could not bring herself to look at him at all. She watched her own hands as they completed their task, then she clutched the sides of her gown and lifted her face to his. His face was anguished and she interpreted the look to mean that he dreaded the unveiling as much as she did. "I'm going to close my eyes and if they repulse you, please, just walk away. I will understand."

She let the gown fall off and she stood before him, her hand hanging in shame. She waited for him to say something, anything – to gasp in horror or to turn and walk away. There was nothing – and then she felt it. He began pressing tender kisses to the puckered scar on her left shoulder. He covered every inch of the ugly, raised disfigurement with his lips, even following it down, as it marred the soft, round globe of her breast. She began to tremble. When he had completed his labor of love on the front, he turned her around and kissed the angry red scar on her back. Turning her back around, he knelt in front of her and placed his head against her body. "Don't you remember where these scars came from?" He took a ragged breath. She said nothing and he continued. "The bullet that tore into your flesh was meant for me. I don't count these marks as scars; they are a visible testament to the fact that you were willing to sacrifice your life for mine. How could I be repulsed by the evidence of so great a gift?" She cradled his head in her arms and felt the dampness of his tears.

He stood to his feet and he picked her up easily as if she were a child. He carried her to their bed and he gently laid her down. As she watched him with wonder in her heart, he undressed quickly and joined her on the bed. Without another word he began to love her. Weeks of abstinence had fueled his appetite, but he forced himself to be as gentle with her as he possibly could. He pressed his long length against her and ran his hands up and down her body as if ensuring himself that she was safe and whole.

"I've missed you, so." He whispered in her ear as he began to kiss her lips. It seemed he could not get as close to her as he needed to be. He didn't want to crush her, so he laid flat and pulled her over on top of him, always mindful of her injury. Both hands cradled her face and his tongue mated with hers, parodying the rhythm that his loins ached to begin. He urged her up higher in the bed until his mouth could reach her breasts. He began to court her nipples, using his tongue to swirl around each one in turn, laving them into submission, causing the pink areolas to pout and swell. He teased her endlessly, nibbling the swell of her breasts, pressing them together and molding them with his hands as if they were clay to be fashioned into a piece of erotic art.

Arabella endured the teasing as long as she could, he knew what she longed for and he wanted to make her beg. "Please." she gasped. He continued the sensual assault, yet avoided the one sensation that she most desired. "Please, Jade," she urged softly.

"Please, what?" he teased. He wanted to make her say it. She was such a lady; it turned him on for her to enunciate what she wanted him to do to her.

She was past the point of caring, "Suck my nipples, please. Suck them hard!" Her words fanned the flames of his desire and he happily gave her what she asked for. He placed his mouth over one nipple and she pushed downward urging him to take more of her in his mouth. He suckled her breast with fervor, his tongue tickling the nipple even as his lips and mouth applied exquisite pressure. The attention he was giving to her nipples sent an electrifying wave of excitement directly to her desperately empty vagina.

Delicate sounds of pleasure escaped her lips, low husky moans and tiny mewls of surrender. He knew that he could make her come just by breast stimulation alone; but he was starving for her and even now his manhood was clamoring for relief.

Aching to be inside of her, he gently edged her over on

the bed and covered her body with his. Careful of her shoulder he adjusted the pillows to make her comfortable and took the pillow from his side of the bed and placed it under her hips. This tilted her vulva up toward him, giving him an erotic view of her hot, pulsating core. Slowly, both of them watching, he guided the head of his penis to the silky pink opening of her vagina. This was only their second time to make love in the flesh. "Do you want me inside of you, Arabella?"

"Yes," she groaned. "Please, Jade. I ache for you." He pushed the head of his penis inside of her very slowly. She began undulating her hips and moving the muscles of her vagina, seeking to draw more and more of him deep within her. They both watched as his thick, hard penis went deeper and deeper. She lifted her hips and tensed her inner muscles massaging the length of him. This triggered the end of his control. "I can't go slowly anymore Arabella, I want you too much." He lifted both of her legs and put them up over his shoulders. This gave him unbridled access to pump into her as hard and fast as she could stand. She gasped as the pleasure. "Oh God, Jade this feels so good." He watched her face as he loved her. There was no pretense, no fake gasps and groans; only pure, unadulterated enjoyment. This woman was not ice, she was fire. Kate had tolerated their sexual encounters; Arabella was an equal, enthusiastic participant.

"Jade, I want to kiss you, please." He changed their positions so that he was covering her and their faces were touching. She wrapped her legs around his waist and lifted her lips to his. As she kissed him, he felt her inner muscles begin to vibrate in an intense orgasm. She bucked underneath him, causing him to explode inside of her. He continued to pump until the last drop of his ejaculation was shot deep inside of her. He lay down on her, supporting himself with his arms so that he wouldn't crush her. "You are the most wonderful lover." She complimented him.

"How would you know? I am the only lover you have ever had." He was teasing her, but then again, he wasn't.

"I know how you make me feel, even now – I love how

you feel inside of me. You have spent yourself, but your penis is so big and thick that it is still giving me pleasure." Her hips began to move under his and her tight sheath began to massage his ultra sensitive rod. She allowed her hips to move in tight little circles and increased the rhythm of her inner muscles and suddenly he found that his penis was growing, expanding, refilling, becoming harder than it had been before.

"Roll over, baby." She did as he asked. He arranged the pillows so that she could lean over them and he could enter her from the back. This was a totally new experience for her, but she trusted him completely. She let the pillows support her middle and she held herself up with her arms on the other side. Her curvy backend was turned up and waiting on his attention. "You have me as hard as a rock." He reached under her and massaged her vulva to ensure that she was still wet enough to handle him. When he touched her she tensed with desire, he guided his penis into her canal and then he moved his hands around to cup both breasts which dangled heavily in front of the pillows. She gasped with delight. He set the speed on slow and sensuous. Every time he plunged in, he tweaked her nipples. She ground her hips back against him, causing him to laugh with joy. "How do you know how to do these things?"

"Fantasies." That one word almost sent him over the edge. The globes of her breasts were the sexiest handles he had ever held on to. He leaned down and kissed the curve of her back. She arched it, attempting to accommodate his every desire. Her breathing picked up and he knew that she was building to another orgasm. He raised her upright on his member and pulled her smooth back against his chest. He kept one hand on her right breast, maintaining the nipple stimulation that drove her crazy. The other hand slipped down to cover her mound. He found her swollen clitoris and he began to rub it in sensuous circles, round and round as he pounded into her now convulsing body.

"God Jade, I'm coming so hard, so good!" She jerked in his arms and her scream of delight catapulted him to the hardest orgasm that he had ever experienced. He held on to her, enjoying every possible ripple of electric ecstasy that could be drained from the mind-blowing experience. Still holding her back against him, he ran the palms of his hands from her shoulders down to below her thighs and then back again, finding their home as they cupped her breasts and squeezed them, not with frantic desire but with devoted appreciation. Then he tenderly kissed the scar on her back. With grateful fingers he tenderly touched the ridge of scar tissue on her shoulder and then he whispered in her ear, "I love you."

When he said those words, the words that she had been longing to hear, she instantly became completely and utterly still. All of the wonderful sensations that had been washing over her body were suddenly overtaken by a much stronger reaction – absolute and utter relief – he had said that he loved her!

Still connected to him in the most intimate and loving way, she did not attempt to turn around for fear of hurting him, plus she could not bear to break that most precious of connections. She lifted the uninjured arm to touch his cheek and turned her head to meet his lips with her own. "Oh, Jade – I love you so."

He must have known, there was no way it could have been a surprise. She had been telling him that she loved him every day of their acquaintance, in every way possible, with every cell of her body. Still, he reacted as if it were unexpected yet longed for news.

Without precedence, he was amazed to find that for the third time in this love making session that he was as thick and hard as he had ever been in his life. And even though she was replete and in some ways exhausted, she accommodated his needs with the greatest of delight.

****

Evangeline and Arabella watched as Angelique took a piece of Lyle Sessions shirt and fashioned it into a small poppet. She carefully sewed buttons on for eyes and stitched a nose and a mouth. Stuffing the poppet with yew, wormwood, pepper and nettles, they had decided to go beyond the more passive protection charms and delve right into full frontal attack. This typical voodoo/hoodoo charm was meant to bring Lyle Sessions to his knees. Angelique took the poppet and stitched it up around the herbs, then she sat it on a marble slab and proceeded to anoint it with Damnation oil. She lit a black candle and then burned a piece of parchment paper, in which his name and his deeds had been inscribed. Next, he placed the oil drenched likeness in a cast iron cauldron and lit the whole thing ablaze - completely obliterating the charmed likeness of the insane killer. "Soon, he will regret that he was ever born." Angelique whispered.

****

While Arabella was still recuperating, Jade took care of quite a bit of business. He cleaned out Kate's things from his apartment and had them delivered post-haste to her parent's house, just as he had promised. He started keeping hours at his congressional office and even met with his campaign team for a quasi reunion/celebration.

He took time to address a session at the capitol and thank everyone for their prayers and supports. He made appointments and noted the times for several critical votes – all things that a good congressman should do.

He also dealt with a persistent job offer from one of the most prestigious law firms in town, which reiterated their desire to have him join the firm. They left the door wide open, if he ever came to the day when politics did not meet his expectations; they foresaw a mutually beneficial association. Jade wasn't closing any doors, right now he didn't know what he wanted – except for Arabella, of course. He had no real need to work, if he never worked another day in his life, he had enough money to meet all of his needs. The politics was a head-rush, but being governor or even president someday was not something that he couldn't live without. The law firm was quite intriguing, he loved a good argument and he missed the days at college when he had excelled at debate and law had seemed like the career for him.

Politics had turned his head and he felt like he had done

some good down at the capitol. Green issues were not usually his parties forte, but he felt as if he were making some headway with some of the old hats and that one day, maybe, the rest of the state would catch up with their forward thinking capitol.

The meeting with Reese, however, did not go as well as everything else had. "Reese, I really don't want to hear this." Jade stated his position emphatically.

"You're making a huge mistake, Jade. That woman is going to finish you in politics. Your names have already been linked. I'm not saying that she isn't coming out in a favorable light, helping find those murder victims and all, but she will never do as wife material. Arabella Landry is certainly no Kate Thompson."

Jade's blood was about to boil over. He was doing everything he could to contain the anger that was just about to erupt. How dare this sanctimonious son of a bitch say those cruel things about Arabella? "Reese, you're my friend, or at least I thought you were. There is one thing that you need to be aware of: Arabella comes first. Politics means nothing to me, compared to her. If my party can't accept me and Arabella as a team, then I don't want anything to do with the party or their politics. As for Kate Thompson, her name is not worthy to even be in the same sentence as Arabella's. Kate is a cold, calculating icicle, where Arabella is a warm, loving, exciting, giving woman."

"Jade, people are talking. It's starting to get around. They're using the word 'witch'."

If Jade hadn't been so furious, he would have laughed. "Reese, Arabella *is* a witch. A precious, powerful, cute-as-a-button, wand-waving, chanting, card-carrying witch. I don't really blame you for your ignorance; I used to be in about the same shape. But that witch and her family saved my life. They used their considerable powers to resurrect me from, might as well be, dead. I will never be able to repay that family the great debt that I owe them. And if you ever do one thing to hurt Arabella or to let her know this vile shit that you are spewing, I will not only beat the hell out of you, I will give Arabella permission to turn you into a roach." Reese shut up and walked out and Jade took a deep breath and shook his head. Actually, he didn't have any idea if Arabella could turn anyone into a roach, but he suspected that if she really wanted to, she probably could.

Now, all he wanted to do was go home to **Wildflower Way**, back to the heaven of her arms.

****

Tyler Garrison was there when Jade got home and he learned that five bodies had indeed been unearthed from the Townsend property. The remains seemed to vary in time as to how long they had been buried; some looked to be years old and others possibly less. There were newspaper reporters and TV cameras everywhere. The road in front of **Wildflower Way** was congested with traffic. News was fast spreading across the state that a serial killer was lurking in the wilds of the Texas Hill Country.

Before Tyler left, he got Jade off to one side. "Congressman, I've looked into your background," he began. "I see that you have a concealed handgun permit."

"I do. I haven't taken advantage of that, I don't exactly think that a servant of the State should walk around on public property armed to the teeth."

"I couldn't agree with you more," the detective acquiesced. "The less people we have walking around with guns, the better I feel – but here and now – I'd feel a lot better if you were armed. Sessions is not going to rest until he kills one of these women and you and I both have a vested interest in keeping them and those they love safe. I hope you don't mind, but I took the liberty of having one of your staff go by your apartment and bring me your weapon."

Jade laughed as he watched the detective bring out Jade's own pistol from his pocket. "If I didn't like you Garrison, this might make me mad. But, I'm with you, this thing with Sessions is not over and I want to do everything I can to protect Arabella and her family." He took his gun from the detective and tucked it into his belt, under his coat.

****

That night in their bed, Jade tried to show her what she really meant to him. Over and over again, the words of Reese Philips echoed in his mind and he strove to apologize to Arabella for other people's ignorance with every kiss of his lips and every stroke of his tongue. She, despite her witchy powers, had no idea that anything was wrong at all. She laughed and played and pleased him endlessly with her soft touch and soft lips and the soft sweet folds of her womanhood.

She lay on his broad chest and stroked the smooth muscles that rippled beneath her touch. She rose up on one elbow and just looked at him. "I cannot get enough of you. Look at this chest," she marveled. "It is so wide and sexy that it . . . .it's just a playground for my fingers (she stroked his nipples with the tips of her fingers) a playground for my tongue (she began to taste him with tiny little licks, like a cat treating himself to cream) a playground for my breasts (she raised up so that her nipples were just grazing his sensitive skin, enflaming his passion once more). He took all that he could, then he twirled her over, and before she knew she had moved, he rammed his hard cock deep into her soft center. He felt the tiniest of flinches and immediately remorse halted his thrusts, "Oh, Arabella, did I hurt you – I should have prepared you, ... " She stopped his words with her lips.

"Hush." She wound her legs around his hips and her arms around his neck and lifted her hips to meet his thrusts. "You didn't hurt me; you just surprised me, that's all." She didn't allow him to stop; rather she made it impossible for him to stop as she began those magical movements that drove him wild. After their loving, he held her until she went to sleep. He vowed to be more careful with her. Despite the male pride that came from knowing he had an extra-large penis, came the responsibility to make sure his love was always ready to accept him.

Then a thought occurred to him that ought to occur to any male over the age of eighteen, if he is sexually active and cares anything about the woman he is sleeping with. He knew their circumstances had been unique, but that did not give him even an iota of an excuse. He was shocked to admit that it had never crossed his mind, not even once in all the glorious times that he had loved her body, to protect her against pregnancy.

☾* ~ Chapter XIII ~ *☽

Something was eating Lyle Sessions. His skin burned and itched. Hiding out in the damned countryside had not been his original plan. Why was the Lord testing him so? Had he not fulfilled his calling? Oh yes, but not with the witches. They still walked free and unencumbered – while he – the Lord's anointed – slunk and hid like a cast away dog.

He clawed at the blisters that rose on his arms and legs. Must have got into a patch of damn poison ivy. Didn't think there was any of that shit this time of year. Soon, it would be over and then he would be free.

****

Tyler finally got a break. Three of the five women had been identified. One of them had been from Houston, a Margie Raddison. She had been a single mother that had disappeared on Interstate 35 at a gas station. A speeding ticket in Sessions name had popped up on the computer and put him less than two miles from the incident within minutes of the abduction. "Shit," Tyler swore. The woman had probably been in the trunk when the officer had been giving the old bastard the speeding ticket. The more information the coroner's pulled from the women's remains, the more convinced they became that Session had given them an injection to knock them out so they would be easily transported and remain manageable until he could get them back to his place.

Yet, despite everything that Detective Garrison and his men had done, Lyle Sessions remained elusive. He had posted officers to watch his home, **Wildflower Way**, his church and every other place that they could spare a man to survey a likely target area. It was as if he had dropped off the face of the earth. Tensions were running high at the herb farm and he knew for their sake, as well as his own that something had to give. When it did, Tyler Garrison had every intention of proposing to Elizabeth Landry.

****

Arabella was happier than anyone had a right to be. Her mother was blossoming under the attention of the now constantly underfoot detective. Dr. Francois had given Jade an absolutely clean bill of health and had talked a normally aloof Angelique into actually going out on the town. It wouldn't surprise Arabella to find out that he was looking into transferring his practice to New Orleans.

Nanette had relented and allowed Evangeline to enroll at the University of Texas for the next semester and she had been busy getting all the paperwork done to have all of her records and hours transferred from Tulane. Nanette, herself, was still immersed in casting spell after spell to protect them and to stop Lyle Sessions from doing anyone else the slightest bit of harm.

As for herself and Jade, Arabella thought that there was no way it could be better. Jade spent his nights at ***Wildflower Way*** and his days in Austin. He had taken up his Congressional mantle and she had begun a scrapbook of all the articles in the newspapers and magazines that covered his service and his bright future.

Arabella was so in love with Jade, that she literally walked around in a euphoria of happiness. She delighted in doing things for him, preparing his meals, taking care of his clothes and satisfying him in bed. She wondered if every woman was as deeply affected by their lover as she was. During the day while they were apart, he would cross her mind and instantly just the thought of him would almost bring her to her knees. Her vagina would feel like an open chasm of emptiness and all she could think about was him filling her, stretching her, bringing her to an earth shattering mind numbing release. She would probably never admit it to him, but sometimes when she was showering, thoughts of him would fill her and she would find herself plucking at her own nipples and thrusting her fingers between her own legs trying to relieve the torment of their separation.

Not that he ignored her in any way. On the contrary,

their nights were full of passion and tender loving. She had noticed that he had begun to wear a condom when they made love. When she first watched him stop before he mounted her, and put on the condom to protect her, she had felt ashamed because she had not been the one to take steps to prevent a pregnancy.

Before Jade, it had never been an issue. She had no female problems or hormone issues that would warrant a prescription for a pill. After Jade, the joy had flowed at such a level that she never let her mind wander beyond the sheer thrill of loving him to consider the possibility of pregnancy. She now realized the foolishness of such an act.

The sight of him taking the small gold packet and stopping to stretch the rubber over his immense penis, she had felt conflicting emotions. At first it was a sight to behold: she had doubts that the rubber would fit over his throbbing rod – she so wanted to help him – any excuse to run her hungry fingers over his velvet cock. Then second thoughts had emerged later, after the loving – did he not want to have a baby with her?

She did not have the courage to mention it to him. It would have seemed logical that she would be confident enough in his love and secure enough in their relationship to broach any subject with him. Jade gave her absolutely no reason to feel otherwise. He was perfect – a considerate, protective, loving, gentle man. Nevertheless, the little niggling doubts remained.

He had never mentioned marriage. Arabella told herself that it didn't matter. She was perfectly happy, just as things were. And she was. But still, to be asked to be his wife would be the pinnacle of joy.

It was odd, but Arabella could not read Jade's mind at all. She could not read anything he touched or foresee any action that he might take. In some ways, she was very grateful for that, but to know how he felt about these things would alleviate a lot of her questions.

Whatever questions or worries she might have, did not for a moment detract from the love she felt for him, or the joy she experienced while they were together. Elizabeth, seer that she was, had honed in on some of her concerns. She, unlike Arabella, could read Jade's thoughts. Most of the time, she tried to be good and stay out of her family's brain, especially now, since she had Tyler to occupy her mind. But every once in a while a vivid picture or a phrase would leap into her thoughts and she would just know what the other person was thinking or feeling.

That afternoon, Elizabeth got the chance to speak to her daughter alone. Arabella was in the drying house mixing up a batch of arthritis tincture when Elizabeth found her. Jade had not come home from work and everyone else was otherwise occupied. "Hey, sweetheart, how are you feeling?"

"Just great, mom." And it wasn't a lie, Arabella was content.

"Is there anything you'd like to talk about, baby?" Arabella marveled at how vivacious and young her mother looked. She only hoped that she had inherited those qualities from her.

"Like what, the murders?"

"No, let's talk something much nicer than – let's talk about your Jade."

At the mention of his name, her heart skipped a beat. A smile danced across her features, she just couldn't help but show the great love that she felt for him. "What about Jade, Mama?"

"I know that you are going through a couple of things, I'm not saying you're not happy – because obviously you are." Her daughter was watching her warily. "What I am saying is that you have questions and I – well, I have answers."

Arabella couldn't help but laugh, "Well, of course you do. What do you think I want to know?"

"First of all, deep down inside, you wonder why, if he loves you so much that he hasn't asked you to marry him?" Arabella didn't move a muscle – there was no use – this was her mother – there was no use denying anything.

"Okay."

"Arabella, Jade loves you with all of his heart. I hear his thoughts and they are the purest that I have ever heard. I have never picked up on the least inkling of dissatisfaction, unhappiness, cold feet, interest in other women – absolutely nothing."

Arabella couldn't help but smile. "I can't say I'm sorry to hear that. What else?"

"He is using protection for just that – to protect you – not because he doesn't want a child with you someday."

Elizabeth placed her arms around her daughter. "I'm not butting in, sweetie. I just hear your concerns loud and clear and I also hear his honest, sweet little thoughts and I couldn't stand you worrying yourself to death for nothing."

"Thanks, mama. That means a lot."

"Actually, for a politician he is quite a surprise. There is not a hint of guile, greed or ambition. I sense only a pure heart and a desire to serve. Now, I do have my suspicions – I bet that loving you has gone a long way in making him this knight in shining armor. He is so happy; he doesn't have time to worry about being bad." She whacked her mother upside the head with a bunch of dried lavender, laughing at Elizabeth's slip into sarcasm.

****

When Jade came home, Arabella met him at the door with open arms and a more peaceful heart. Tyler was back over for dinner so they had an enjoyable family meal – only Angelique was missing and that was fine, because she was out with the debonair Dr. Francois. The only thing that marred their good time was the black cloud of Lyle Sessions that hung over their head.

The family had become adept at making themselves scarce so Jade and Arabella could have time alone. They seemed to realize that the few hours between bedtime and midnight were not enough for all of the small talk, dream sharing, hand holding and mind-blowing sex that the couple craved. Their bedroom had become their haven – their world away from the world. Today was no different.

"This bill that I've been working on is really going to make a difference for a lot of college students. Some of us are trying very hard to freeze the tuitions so that getting a good education is not such a burden on our students."

"I know that Evangeline would appreciate that. Tell me more." Arabella laid on her side on the bed, facing the sexy hunk that, unbelievably, belonged to her.

"Another bill that I am sponsoring would bypass the governor's attempt to refuse the additional stimulus funds that will help our state's unemployed." Arabella was trying to listen, she really was – but all she could think about while she watched Jade talk was how much she would love to kiss those sweet lips of his. She tensed one leg against the other trying to fight down the sexual tension that was already building between her thighs. She so wanted to be everything that he needed in a woman, but sometimes all she wanted was him – hot, and hard and all night long. 'Stop it' she fussed at herself. She refocused her eyes on his face and then she realized that he was watching her with the slightest of smiles. He knew! He was getting as bad as her mother!

He decided to tease her a bit. "Is there something that I can do for you, Arabella?" She wasn't about to make it that easy for him. No use to give him the big head. Ohhhhh, even that thought made her quiver – his head was big – both of them, actually. She was melting, right where the heat sizzled in the hot pool between her legs!

"I'm not sure what you mean, Jade. There's nothing that I need from you. I am completely self sufficient." He began to lean toward her, moving in the slowest of increments.

"Are you saying you don't need anything, sweetheart? You can take care of yourself, is that it?" Only a fraction of electrified air separated their lips, but he was going to make her come to him – if only that last, little distance. Oh, she tried – it would do him good – if she could just roll over and pretend to be interested in a movie – it would do him good – if she could just make him think for a moment that he wasn't the most irresistible stud on the planet. But he knew better – and so did she. He stopped that small distance away from her and the look in his eyes could have melted rock. "Come to me, Arabella."

These were the same words that he had first said to her in their dream. They were the most precious words in the English language. Every bone in her body melted and she closed the distance instantly, cuddling up to him, giving herself to him, making everything that she had available to his kiss and to his touch. She was so ready for him, she had been all day. Clothes were stripped off and pushed to the floor. Thinking that this would be the one time when his tantalizing, infuriating control would be lost – she was wrong. He sat up in the bed and rested his back against the solid head board. Mystified, she let him turn her around until she sat between his thighs with her back leaning on the flat, hard, mountain that was his chest. It made her feel so small and helpless, it was dramatically exciting.

She was facing away from him, but she was totally at his mercy and the only part of him that she could reach was his oak-hard legs that framed her and embraced her. His hands began their torment. They started at her neck, lifting her hair so that he could kiss the curve of her neck and tease the shell of her ear. He gently rubbed her shoulders, like the tenseness in her body had anything at all to do with her shoulders – she just might scream. . . . Then he stroked both muscular hands down her arms and with feathery light touches brought them back up. Then his hands began their torture of her breasts. It hadn't taken him very long to find out how to absolutely drive her mad. Her breasts and nipples were the hot button area of her body – not that her loins did not scream out for him – it did – but she adored how he worshipped her breasts. She laid her head back on his shoulder and swooned. He circled them, cupped them, and weighed them with his hands. He lifted them, massaged them, rubbing the nipples between his fingers until she screamed with joy. And just as soon as she thought he was through, he would begin again. This time, he pushed her all the way. Not a finger went any lower than the underside of her breasts and he made her orgasm – trembling, her hips pumping up and down, giving themselves the only stimulation that he would allow. She arched her neck and begged for his mouth and he met her lips and kissed them reverently as she shook with the richness of her climax.

"More," she whispered into his mouth.

"You are insatiable, witch." When he said the word, he might as well have said the word angel – because it was said with all the depth of feeling that he possessed. His hands encircled her breasts once more and then they both moved lower. He put one on either side of her most tender flesh and pulled her tightly back against him. She could feel the rock hard presence of his penis that was right behind her hips and nestled against her lower back. It was so big, it seemed to reach to her shoulder blades – and it was getting bigger by the second.

He spread her legs wide against his own and then both hands occupied themselves between her thighs. One hand went toward the place of her greatest need, the emptiness that she had longed for him to fill all day. And he filled it with one finger and then two. The other hand massaged and manipulated her clitoris. The double onslaught drove her mad. No matter how his own sex begged to be an active participant, he kept up the invasion at the entrance to paradise. She didn't really know what a G-spot was, but she knew when he found it. The combination of the measured insistent finger thrusts and the constant, circular petting of her clitoris drove her into a frenzy. She writhed in ecstasy, she bucked, she rocked against his hand, she threw both arms over her head and around his neck and she thought that she would die from the longest, hottest release imaginable.

Best of all, it was only just the beginning. Now, Jade would give her what she really wanted all along. His hands and fingers had brought her pleasure, but what she wanted most was between his legs. He laid her down and he brought himself over her – their eyes were locked together. He leaned back until he could fit the condom over his cock and then he spread her legs wide and eased himself into her. He marveled at how impossibly tight she was. Her muscles were toned and strong, she had incredible muscle control -- and his raging rod loved it. Slowly he pushed down into her moist, hot depths. Her inner muscles hungrily grasped him – inch over inch.

When they first began making love, he had known she was more responsive than any woman that he had ever been with – but now that she had tasted the complete banquet - she was beyond belief in bed. Jade did not know what he had ever done to deserve such a treasure. It wasn't something that you bragged about, but he would have liked to shout it from the rooftops – his woman was a wildcat in bed! She enjoyed him and she had no problem letting him know it. She fed his ego more than anyone ever had. When he was completely buried within her, he watched her face. Her eyes closed with the sheer pleasure of it, her sweet hips lifted off of the bed and she began to rock him and stroke him. "I've been dreaming about this all day." she whispered. So had he. He didn't have to move at all – but he wanted to. He let her enjoy herself just a moment longer and then he took over. He sat up and pulled her up in his lap, with her head still back on the pillow but her hips across his thighs. Her legs crossed behind his back. He braced himself and began thrusting. Over and over again, deeper and deeper. Arabella began to moan and grabbed the bottom sheet on the bed and held on to it for dear life.

Still he kept pumping into her, slamming against her thighs in the ancient, pagan, rhythm of life. He climbed the mountain of passion and when he reached the crest he shouted triumphantly and drove into her one final time – as his magnificent body shuddered with the force and excitement of his climax. She allowed herself to join him and ride the overwhelming tidal wave of passion until they lie spent and replete in each other's arms.   "Bella, My God, Bella – you are mine – no one else will ever love you – no one else will ever know how wild and exciting you are."

"Jade, it's only for you. If we had not met, I would have never known any of his. I would still be the twenty four year old virgin, waiting for life to pass her by."

Jade did not like to think what might have been. They

were together and that was all that mattered.

****

The next day Jade called from work, she had been about to leave for the Post Office to mail some packages. It was unusual for him to call during the day, so she knew something special was up. "Arabella, I know its January, but the temperature outside is more like April. How would you like to have a noon picnic up on Enchanted Rock with me?"

He didn't expect her to disagree and she didn't disappoint him. "It sounds like heaven. I'll pack a lunch, what time are you picking me up?"

"Eleven thirty and dress warmly." Their lives were so busy that they had not spent much time together away from *Wildflower Way*. Their hunger for one another was so overpowering that this venture outdoors was unusual and Arabella found it quite exciting. She packed thick turkey and Swiss sandwiches, fried some wafer thin, homemade potato chips and made Jade's favorite chocolate oatmeal cookies. She knew that he would have been satisfied with whatever she could have found in the fridge, but she took every chance to spoil him that she could.

Evangeline and Elizabeth went to the post office for her and she dressed as he requested and sat down to wait on him. She had glanced at the calendar and today was a very special day. It was the day of the full moon, the second full moon of the month – a wishing moon – and if she had only one wish to make in her life it would be this – she asked for the wisdom and the strength to make Jade Landale happy.

****

Jade had the whole thing planned out to the nth degree. The week before, he had combed the finest jewelry stores in Austin until he had located the perfect diamond engagement ring. It was almost as beautiful as Arabella. Five carats of perfect diamond were set in a classic, yet simple gold setting. He looked at the ring every few minutes, hoping that she would love it.

The decision to ask her to marry him had been simmering beneath his consciousness for weeks. He had been in love with her even before he had left ***Tranquility***, even before he had actually met her, if the truth be known. Jade closed up the office, placed the ring box in his pocket and slid into his silver Aston Martin.

When he arrived at ***Wildflower Way***, she did not wait for him to come in. Watching out the window, she saw him coming and ran out to meet him, picnic basket in hand. He marveled at how beautiful she was in a winter white pantsuit with a smart little hood to catch the waterfall of dark silky hair.

She joined him in the car and immediately reached for a kiss. There was no doubt where he stood with Arabella, Kate had been notorious for throwing temper tantrums and pouting endlessly, making him work for every morsel of affection she doled out to him. Arabella was lavish in her affection and constant in her love – there was no put on or deception. Arabella was genuinely sweet and considerate.

"I can't wait to be on top of Enchanted Rock with you." she smiled at him.

"Arabella, I very much doubt that we'll be able to do . . . . ,"

She stopped him, embarrassed. "Oh, that's not what I meant – I would never expect you to make a spectacle of yourself for me. I know you are a public figure." She sounded so contrite that he was sorry he had teased her.

"I was just joking, baby. Making love to you would never embarrass me, the only thing that I refuse to do is ever allow you to be put into a situation where other men will see or enjoy what belongs only to me."

"Stop, Jade." For a moment, he thought she was angry, but then heat rose in him when he realized that she was turned on. She sat very still with her eyes closed. He was tempted to pull over on the side of the road and pleasure her until she screamed. But he was on a mission and the sex – and he knew it would be great – would have to wait until they returned home. But when they returned home, she would be wearing his ring.

****

They walked up the Summit Trail hand in hand. He

carried the basket and enjoyed himself, just watching her having a good time. When they arrived at the top of the dome, he would have given anything if they had it to themselves, but of course they did not. They walked around the wide pink granite mountain. "Do you remember the first time we met in the dream, Jade? I do, it had been a lonely day for me. I had worked hard trying to catch up on all the holiday orders and the only company I had all week were the cats and the constant barrage of emails. I remember going to bed and wishing that I had somebody to hold. Sometimes, I would hug my pillow and pretend that I was not alone.' He listened patiently to her as she opened her heart to him. "This is going to sound strange, but I believe I dreamed about you many times before that night. I never could see your face, but that first time I kissed you – I recognized you. You have been in my dreams all of my life."

He couldn't stand it any longer. He sat the picnic basket down and kissed her with all the passion and tenderness that welled up from his soul. He held her tight and stroked her back and thanked the Gods that Arabella Landry belonged to him. He was about to reach in his pocket and take out the diamond engagement ring, suddenly, she stiffened. Every nerve in her body was on red alert – and this time it wasn't passion. He looked down at her and saw that she was looking just past his right shoulder. He was much too tall for her to see over his shoulder so he realized that she had become aware of something just to the right of him. "Jade, be very still. Lyle Sessions is behind you and he has a gun. Oh, god – there are other people up here – Jade this could turn into a massacre." She made the slightest of movements; incredibly, he realized that she was about to once again step around to place herself between him and the attacker, as she had done before.

"Not again, Bella, not again." Jade heard the crazy old man cock the deer rifle. Thanking Tyler Garrison with everything that was in him, he whirled around pulling the pistol out as he turned and just as soon as he could distinguish Sessions from any innocent bystander, he fired a bullet straight into the old man's wicked, black heart.

****

Lyle Sessions was dead before he hit the ground and Jade hoped that the God that this maniac thought he served sent him straight to the hottest pits of hell. Arabella was so weak with relief and terror that she had to sit down on the cold, damp granite. The park rangers had been on the top of the rock in minutes and had called the police and the EMS. They helped him get Arabella down off of the dome and into the relative warmth of the park station house. She was trembling uncontrollably; Jade had never seen her so upset. "It's over Bella. You don't have to be afraid, I'm here with you."

"I know." She tried to explain. "I'm not afraid – well that's not true – for just a moment I saw what could have been. Nanette and Angelique's magic and your quick thinking and action saved us, but for a moment fate let me see what could have happened. I saw you fall – I saw you cut down by that crazy old fool. All I could think about was that he was after me – not you – never you – Oh, God I put you in danger again. What if he had shot you?" She was crying, his heart was breaking and the ring was forgotten.

"Bella, its okay – what might have been – it never will be." He held her close, rocking her, kissing the top of her head until Tyler Garrison arrived to take their statements and then let them go home.

****

When they finally made it back to **Wildflower Way**, Arabella had calmed down. Tyler had called the family and they were all waiting in the living room for Arabella and both men to arrive. Gratitude and thanksgiving was on everyone's lips. The nightmare was finally over.

Tyler tried to give them something of an explanation. "When they took Lyle Sessions down off of E-Rock they found a small notebook in his pocket, where he had written down ramblings that somewhat explain his actions. It seems that years ago, he had an unrequited love for Rachel

Townsend. They attended church together and even though they shared a pew, Rachel was not interested in sharing anything else. It appears that he became obsessed with her and if you look at the pictures of all the women he killed, they were very similar in looks to how Rachel Townsend appeared through the years. He killed Kathy and Lea because they weren't his child and grandchild. The lack of love warped that old man into a killer. He convinced himself that he was doing the Lord's will in eradicating society of women who, as far as he was concerned, were temptations sent by God to punish mankind.'

"That's sick." Evangeline said what everybody else thought.

"Tyler, I sure am glad you brought that gun to me. If you hadn't, it would have just been a replay of what happened before, but this time one of us or both of us would have died."

Elizabeth hugged Tyler and thanked the gods that he had enough wisdom to prepare for what was to come.

****

The next day, Angelique and Nanette drove Evangeline to her new dorm room in Austin. Then, they headed back to the Big Easy. Elizabeth invited Tyler Garrison to spend a few days with her in Galveston; after all he had certainly earned a vacation.

Jade talked Arabella into coming to his Austin loft for the weekend – just for a change of scenery. She thought that was a good idea. Her nerves were still so on edge that she didn't feel like she wanted to be by herself for very long. Jade had promised that if she would come to Austin, they would take in the town. He had promised her a trek down 6th street, tickets to a community theater and to eat out anywhere that she wanted. Little did he know that *he* was all that she wanted.

Arabella put the cats out plenty of food and made sure that all the plants had a good drink of water before she left. She hadn't spent a night away from her home in almost three years. Her house, it seemed was the drawing card in the family, so they had all gravitated to **_Wildflower Way_** for every vacation and every holiday.

When she stepped into his beautiful loft, she saw Kate Thompson everywhere she looked. Forcing that from her mind, she followed him to his huge bedroom. It dwarfed the room that they had been occupying, and to tell the truth, all of the beautiful expensive things intimidated her somewhat.

Jade did not notice her trepidation; all he could think about was setting the stage and making it perfect, so he could ask her to be his wife.

❰* ~ Chapter XIV ~ *❱

Arabella looked out the window of Jade's apartment at downtown Austin. The pink granite dome of the capitol building was to the right - made from the same material as their own special place, E-Rock - and the infamous, yet beautiful tower that stood guard on the University of Texas campus stood to the left. Austin was an exciting place. When she had been at *Wildflower Way*, it had been easy to ignore what an important figure that Jade actually was in Texas politics. Here, it wasn't so easy. There had been three phone calls so far tonight, all requesting his presence at some reception or cocktail party to honor one dignitary or another. She had assured him that they could attend anything that he thought was necessary, she knew that she would have to hurriedly purchase a suitable dress – but that could be done.

Jade had turned down all the invitations. She hoped that he wasn't short-changing himself on any necessary networking opportunities. It would break her heart if she were the one that was responsible for holding him back in anyway. To Arabella, it didn't really matter what they did. She would be content at a party, a restaurant, or just staying here at his beautiful apartment – as long as they were together.

Jade had it all planned out. Tonight was Friday and they were both worn out from the harrowing pressure they had been under. So he had planned a romantic evening at home. They had never had the luxury of a house all to themselves before and he intended to take full advantage of that. He had a bottle of Dom Perignon on ice and had arranged for a romantic meal to be catered right to his dining table.

Tomorrow was a different story, however. He had tickets for a University of Texas college theater performance. Evangeline would be there and even though it wouldn't be the most romantic of situations – Jade knew that Arabella would love being with her cousin and seeing her enjoy the college that she had always wanted to attend. Evangeline was especially eager for Arabella to meet one of the actors in the play; she swore he was a young, Elvis Presley look-a-like, with enough southern charm to melt honey on a winter's day. He had been her Orientation Adviser when she had visited the campus a few weeks ago and they had instantly hit it off.

After that, Jade planned to take Arabella out for a romantic dinner at Aquarelle Restaurant Francais, Austin's premier gourmet French restaurant. There, he planned to ask her to marry him. He couldn't wait to see her face when he gave her the ring. But that was tomorrow – now, he intended to thoroughly enjoy the present.

****

Jade waited on Arabella hand and foot. He wouldn't let her do a thing. She dug her toes into the luxurious, thick, off-white pile carpeting and marveled at how spotless and perfect everything was. The carpet wasn't the only white thing in the room. The massive sectional sofa was white, the marble around the fireplace was white and the coffee table and end tables seemed to be also made from thick, pale granite set in ornate wrought iron. She could just imagine her cats stepping around on this museum quality furniture tracking itty bitty pieces of cat litter on their not so clean paws. The cats would have to stay at **Wildflower Way**.

She nestled back into the corner of the huge sofa. Jade was getting crystal glasses from the kitchen and had turned on a television that was the size of a theater screen. Ripples of desire were competing with twinges of uncertainty. Jade was still Jade, and she worshipped the ground he walked on, but this place was so big and perfect that she felt like the country witch had come to town - and she wasn't dressed properly for it, she knew. She pulled her legs up under her in an involuntary defensive position. She felt so out of place in soft, worn blue jeans and a simple cotton camisole. She played with the buttons on the front of her shirt and longed for Dior, or even Dolce and Gabbana.

Jade reappeared, completely oblivious to her silly discomfort. "I can't believe we are finally alone," he said as he poured her a glass of the renowned champagne. She took it and sipped, enjoying the way the bubbles danced across her nose. "Don't get me wrong - I adore your family - but here, we can make love in the kitchen and on the dining room table, on the rug in front of the TV, on the pool table in the game room - and have you seen the Jacuzzi in the bedroom?" His words made her shiver. "Which one would you prefer?" He smiled at her, eagerly waiting to see which one intrigued her the most.

Her words rocked his world, "All of them, please." He threw back his head and laughed, she was absolutely irresistible.

"I am positive that can be arranged, but first let's do justice to this five hundred dollar bottle of champagne." At the price, Arabella looked dismayed, but he warned her with his eyes to not say a word. He longed to give her the very best of everything. The bubbles went straight to her head, Arabella had not tasted alcohol very often and tonight she was already so high on love that the champagne gave her courage that she had not known she possessed.

She was sitting next to the wide arm of the sofa; the end table was at her side. When he finished the last drop in his glass, she took it from him and set both of the glasses carefully on the table – she knew Waterford when she saw it. Then she took him by one of his wide shoulders and gently pressed him down until she could cradle his head in her lap. Jade had turned the lights on dim and a fire in the fireplace cast dancing shadows around the room. She looked deep into his eyes, conveying all the passion and depth of feeling that a look could possibly give. She laid a gentle hand on his hair and stroked its soft silkiness. With the other hand, she traced his full, sensual mouth, remembering the pleasure that these lips had given her during the weeks that had been together. She then traced his brow and marveled at the rich unique shade of his eyes

– dark greenish brown with a perfect sunburst around the black pupil, making the eyes appear golden and rich like a coin in a fountain. Not a word passed between them, but sometimes words weren't necessary. He slowly unbuttoned her blouse and then unhooked the front closure of her bra. Her breasts spilled out and he captured one already taunt nipple in his mouth. He began to pull on it sensuously with his lips. Every tug at her breast was echoed by a tug in her loins. His left hand worked the other breast, giving her such pleasure that her toes began to curl. Several times, she tried to stop him, so they could move on to things that she knew would bring him pleasure, but he persisted, deriving almost as much satisfaction from the suckling and laving as she did.

She stood it as long as she could, but she finally gave in to the temptation to lay her hand over the huge bulge in his jeans and begin her own brand of sweet torture. As he sucked, she rubbed and molded and stroked him through his pants. He wasn't wearing jeans so the linen fabric gave her much greater access to his manhood than the thick denim fabric would have. He grew impossibly large as she worked him through the soft material. At last, Jade let her nipple slip from his mouth and he rose up to devour her lips. She had him revved up to high gear. His tongue plunged between her lips, coiling around her own, letting her know that his control was fast slipping away.

They had never made love on a couch before and even though this couch was big, Jade opted for a place with more surface area. He picked her up and laid her down on the thick rug in front of the fire. Standing over her he began to undress. His shirt went first, exposing that massive chest that Arabella longed to caress. The pants and under shorts were shed in a minimum of movements and the result of Arabella's handwork came into heart stopping view. He jutted straight out, thick and bold, ready to occupy what he had already conquered.

Arabella did not stay where he placed her. As he stood there, she could not resist rising to her knees to come and pay homage to a part of him that thrilled her beyond belief.

She placed one hand around his shaft and with the other she cupped his steel-hard balls, delicately letting him know, that she adored every part of his body. Her lips closed around the head of his penis and she lovingly swirled her tongue around and around before beginning to take more of him in her mouth. His hand went to the back of her head, pressing her even closer, yet careful not to push himself so far into her mouth that she would experience discomfort. She loved him with all she had, her hands moving up and down the hair roughened muscles of his thighs. She felt his whole body stiffen and the next thing she knew she was flat on her back and her jeans and panties had been thrown to one side.

Always taking care of her, he applied the condom and took time to insure with his fingers that she was as wet as she would need to be to accommodate the raging bull that her lips had created. Finding her soft and ready, he spread her legs wide and lowered himself between them. He was about to guide himself into her when the task was commandeered from him and Arabella, grasping his cock lifted her hips to welcome him home. Sighs of contentment escaped from her lips as he sunk deep within her. It was all he could to maintain a scrap of control as she began to make love to him.

Heat was rising fast and Jade knew that this would not be a night where he could stop and wait for his blood pressure to even out. He was so excited that a few moments of watching her enjoy him, sent him completely over the edge. He raised himself up on his arms and began driving into her with deep sensuous strokes. She elevated her hips so that she had an unhampered view of his member pumping in and out of her vagina. The luscious friction of his pelvic bone against her clitoris caused Arabella to moan with rapture and she began to tremble with release.

The sweet sounds escaping her lips triggered an explosive climax for Jade and he drove himself deep and then ground his member around in a sensuous motion that savored every last spasm of her vagina. Their lips met in a hot, sweet kiss that celebrated the devotion that each had for the other.

****

Friday night was a celebration of love for Arabella and Jade. They had been through so much and now it seemed that all of their problems were behind them and they could begin to just enjoy one another. After their loving, they cuddled on the couch and watched a family movie about a dog – soon she was in tears and he had the best time comforting her, wiping her eyes and making her blow her nose.

The food that Jade had delivered was scrumptious. Austin was known for its Barbeque and Jade was so amused to watch her lick sauce from the corners of her mouth only to find that it was all over her cheeks and nose and fingers. He enjoyed cleaning her up.

Never let it be said that he disappointed her. He made love to her on the granite countertop in the kitchen – finding that it was just the right height for him to enter her standing flat-footed on the marble floor, cradling her head on his shoulder with her legs wrapped around his waist. He made love to her in the wide Jacuzzi bathtub, utilizing the tantalizing water from the jets to drive her crazy. Then he made love to her in his bed, laying claim to the most precious possession that he had ever found – the love of Arabella Landry.

****

Saturday morning, Jade received a phone call that he wasn't expecting. He apologized profusely but there was a quick meeting that he had to make time for. He told her to remain in the bed and he would be back before she knew it.

She tried to do as he said, but the big bed held no attraction for her once he had left it. Making herself at home, she showered and dressed. The door bell startled her and she ran to the door, thinking maybe Jade was on the other side waiting to surprise her – returning far sooner than he had expected.

She was a bit startled to find Reese Phillips standing there. "Hello Reese," she greeted him cordially. "Jade isn't here, but he will be back shortly if you would like to wait."

He stepped through the door a few feet and then he let her have it. "I see it didn't take you long to make yourself right at home."

Arabella didn't understand his tone. "It's a very beautiful apartment."

Reese walked on into the living room expecting her to follow. "I don't have a lot of time, Miss Landry, so let me come right to the point."

What was this about? Suddenly, she would have given anything for Jade to walk through the door. She didn't think this man would try and hurt her, but she was very afraid of what he was about to say.

"I would appreciate it if you would." Arabella gave him permission to speak.

"Jade Landale has a bright future in Texas politics, maybe even on the national scene. I have worked tirelessly to ensure that he meets all the right people and has every opportunity to go as far and rise as high as he wants to. He is talented and has just the right charisma and frankly there is nothing standing between him and the governor's mansion, but you."

Arabella didn't say a word.

"You are toxic to his chances to succeed. You will never fit in with the movers and the shakers in the party. He had the right woman, and I know that accident was partly responsible for their breakup – but he will never succeed with a new-age bimbo like you on his arm."

"I would never do anything to hold Jade back."

"You don't have to do anything, it's already begun. Your name has been linked with his several times over the last month. I'm already getting phone calls. You make people nervous. Witchcraft and family values don't mix."

Arabella wanted to tell him that her family had very good values, but she knew there would be no convincing him of that. "I won't stand in his way, Mr. Phillips. I don't force Jade to stay with me."

"What do you mean, lady – you bought and paid for him twice? I don't know what role you played in his recovery, but he gives you and your family full credit. And then you go and take a bullet for him – my God – he will never leave you. But be aware; gratitude makes a rocky foundation for marriage. Has he proposed to you yet?"

She shook her head, no.

"Well, doesn't that tell you anything? He is with you simply because he doesn't know how to walk away from you. He owes you too much!"

As Arabella's heart broke into a million pieces, she had to confess to herself that Reese Phillips made perfect sense. She hung her head in defeat.

Reese had the good grace to begin to feel remorse for the beautiful woman that stood before him, and he had to admit that she was sexy as hell. "Look, I know you love Jade. I know you would do anything for him – God, you've certainly proved that. But if you really love him, the greatest gift you could ever give him – is to just walk away. Give him his freedom and let him go back to the life that he had before the accident, before he ever met you – let Jade go back to where he belongs."

With that Reese Phillips was gone.

****

When Jade returned to the loft, he entered the door juggling a bouquet of beautiful white lilies and what he thought was a romantic lunch – a loaf of artisan bread, a wedge of creamy Brie, a bunch of sweet red grapes and a pricey bottle of French wine. All he could do was think of ways to spoil Arabella. While he had been in that useless meeting, listening to a lobbyist drone on and on about the dangers of same-sex marriage – Jade had been making a list of places he would like to take Arabella and things that he wanted them to do together. He had thought of taking her swimming at the Austin landmark natural spring, 'The Blue Hole', when it got warmer, of course. Before that, he thought how gorgeous she would be in a tight ski outfit and how much fun she would have romping through the snow. The list had gone on and on, but the last thing that he had written down was to take her to Paris on their honeymoon and walk with her under the stars next to the lazy Seine.

He wanted to give her the world, and tonight, after she accepted his proposal they would begin to make plans.

"Arabella, I'm home." He was so used to her unbridled joy every time she saw him, that when she did not answer him – he instantly knew something was wrong. Slinging the groceries and flowers on the dining table, he ran to the bathroom, thinking she might have fallen and hit her head in the shower.

She wasn't there.

He searched every room in his loft and she was just nowhere. He plowed his hand through his hair, trying to remember if she had said anything about going anywhere. He was about to call Evangeline to see if she had went to her cousin's dorm when he saw the note.

It was propped up on his pillow, on top of the neatly made bed. His hands trembled as he picked it up.

Dearest Jade

I have been so selfish. You have to realize that it was not intentional. I would never do anything to hurt you, but sadly it appears that I have. Your assistant came to visit me this morning and he was kind enough to point out to me that I am not the woman you need. I've already hurt your career and I pray that it is not beyond salvaging. If I had known that our paths would cross, I would have lived my life differently and molded myself into the type of person that you could be proud of – a woman that would be an asset to you instead of a liability.

Please forgive me for not seeing it for myself. I have so enjoyed loving you. I will never forget or regret even one second that we spent together. Thank you for showing me what it meant to be loved by a kind and generous man.

I know that you are grateful to me for the part I was permitted to play in your health and well-being. Mr. Reese made it clear that gratitude is no reason to be tied to someone for life. He's right. I know that you're too wonderful to ever willingly hurt me and I want to assure you that I walk away with the best of memories.

Thank you for letting me love you. Please succeed and be happy.

Bella

Jade bellowed his fury and frustration. He was going to kill Reese Phillips with his bare hands! Abandoning his lunch offerings on the table, he grabbed the flowers and headed for his car. He had no idea how Arabella had left, she didn't have a vehicle.

First, he called Evangeline, but he could tell instantly she knew nothing. He was polite, but he didn't take time to explain. Next, he called Elizabeth.

"Hello, sweetie. You've got yourself into a pickle, haven't you?"

"Where is she Elizabeth?" His voice sounded tight and desperate.

"She's on her way back home. I talked to her for just a second and she said she was taking a cab. I've never heard her sound so desolate."

"How did this happen, how could she believe that fool assistant of mine – haven't I shown her I love her with every breath in my body?"

Elizabeth's heart was breaking for him. He really did love her daughter. "You did nothing wrong, Jade. The doubts were already there, fostered from years of prejudice and self-righteous attitudes. Arabella has gone through things that you had no way of knowing. She has borne the brunt of being brought up in a family that chose to walk a different path than everyone else."

"What do I do?" Elizabeth could hear the tears that were just beneath the surface of his voice.

"Go to her. Do not let her push you away. She won't be expecting you; in her mind you are probably relieved that she finally woke up to the fact that she wasn't right for you. And slow down, it won't do her or you any good if you find yourself wrapped around a telephone pole."

Jade obeyed his future mother in law and let up on the gas. "How do I start – what do I say – how do I convince her that she is the only thing that matters to me?"

"I can't tell you that. The words must be yours. She has to know that you won't feel cheated even if you have to give up politics – because face it, in that respect your assistant is right on the money. Loving Arabella will cost you the governor's mansion."

"Screw the Governor and his mansion."

"That's my boy! Oh, and listen, let me be the first to congratulate you. Arabella doesn't know it yet, but the two of you are going to make me a very young grandmother." With that, Elizabeth hung up the phone.

****

Jade didn't breathe for five miles. Arabella was pregnant? Then, he remembered the times that they had made love before he thought about protecting her. He was overjoyed, but he had no idea how she would feel about it. The Aston Martin ate up the miles, but soon he was on the road that led home. He met a yellow cab going back the way he had come, so he knew that she was there – he could just imagine how she was feeling. Never in his life had he felt so helpless, and so hopelessly afraid that he would not find the right words to say.

He walked up the steps, still carrying the huge bouquet of lilies. He didn't bother to knock. He opened the door and walked in, knowing exactly where to find her. He softly opened the door to their room and stepped through it. No lights were on and the curtains were pulled. She was curled up into a tight knot clutching his pillow in desperation. She had not heard him come in and the last thing that he wanted to do was scare her, he dropped to his knees at the side of the bed and whispered, "Bella."

He saw her whole body jerk, but she didn't turn to him automatically as she always had done before.

"Bella, please come to me."

She still didn't move, but her small voice broke his heart. "Oh, Jade please... please don't make this any harder than it already is. You have to go."

He crawled into bed with her, molding himself around her as if to shield her from any more pain. She stiffened at first, but then he felt her take a deep breath and relax her body back into his embrace. Her body knew what her mind could not accept.

"Where do you want me to go, Bella?" he asked her gently, his breath caressing her soft shell ear.

"I want you to go back to Austin and . . . be happy," she whispered brokenly.

"I can't be happy away from you."

"I'm ruining your chances to be governor, please, please just go – I can't stand to be the cause of you not having what you deserve." Jade began to work the pillow from her grasp. He kissed her on her neck and on the side of her face and told her in no uncertain terms the same thing he had told her mother.

"Screw being governor. What I want is you. I have another job just waiting when this term is over. And if I never worked again, I have enough money to last us through five life times – as long as the price of oil stays high. And if I didn't have one red cent, I would think that I was the richest man in the world if I just had you." She let go of the pillow and she turned in his arms until she was face to face with him. She showered his face with kisses, then buried her head in his neck and clung to him for dear life.

"How could you believe that idiot Phillips?" He asked her gently. "Haven't I shown you how much I love you over and over again? Haven't I worshiped you with my body? Don't you feel loved, Arabella?"

"Yes, but I was afraid that you loved me out of gratitude, I never want you to feel trapped. I want you to stay as long as you want to – not because you feel tied to me."

"I'm grateful to God for you Arabella, but I love you – not out of gratitude – but out of trust, and out of joy, and out of pure unadulterated lust. But, mostly I love you out of the depths of my heart, you came to me out of a dream and it's a dream that I never want to wake up from."

Jade kissed her mouth reverently and then he kissed both eyelids and then he kissed the damp tears from both cheeks. "I have a question to ask you?" He sat up on the bed and he gathered her into his arms. She was as cuddly and warm as a kitten, yet he knew that she possessed powers that he would never understand. He did understand one power that she had – she held his heart in the palm of her very small hand.

Her head was lying on his shoulder and he maneuvered her around until he could reach the ring box in his pocket. When she saw the box, her breath caught in her throat. "I had this with me up on E-Rock. That's why we went on the picnic, but things didn't work out quite like I planned." He kissed her once hard and then he sat her on the bed and he knelt in front of her.

Taking her hand in his, he looked her directly in the eye. "Arabella Landry, witch of my dreams, will you marry me?" He pushed the gold ring on her finger and she looked at it, then at him. It was obvious that no matter how beautiful the ring was or how much she loved it – what she really valued was him.

Not content to be on the bed without him, she joined him on the floor, kneeling in front of him. "You do me the greatest honor, Jade Landale. Yes, I will marry you and I promise to care for you, love you and cherish you every day of my life."

"I'm counting on it."

His closeness was affecting her just as it always had and just as it always would. "I never thought I would be in your arms again." She began unbuttoning his shirt, kissing every inch of flesh she exposed. "I didn't know how I was going to survive without you." She pushed his shirt to one side and delicately licked his nipple. "Will you make love to me now, please?"

He groaned at her sweetness. Pulling her top over her head and quickly ridding her and then himself of all their unnecessary clothes, he adored her with his hands and with his mouth. She arched into him, reveling in his heated caresses. Remembering what Elizabeth had told him, he slowed – leaning over her and tenderly kissing her still very flat stomach. Not knowing what he was up to, she urged him lower, hungry for the feel of his mouth on her quivering clitoris. He did not disappoint her, but lavished her with love until she cried out in passion. She reached for his penis, anxious to sheath him in her warmth. He allowed himself to be led, but entered her with the greatest of care – knowing that his child nestled securely under her heart. He rocked her to ecstasy, cherishing every breath that touched his cheek from her lips.

After the last shiver had been enjoyed to the fullest, he cradled her to him, arranging her so that her head lay on one of his arms and he was lying on his side facing her. He ran his hand over both of her full beautiful breasts and down so that it rested protectively over her womb. "Your mother gave me some news that I would like to share with you."

She was so satisfied and still that he thought for a moment she had dropped off to sleep. At the mention of her mother, though, she opened her eyes, waiting for the other shoe to drop. "Mother gave you news, about me?" 'Mother, what are you up to?' she thought. "When did you talk to Elizabeth?"

"I called my future mother-in-law, the moment that I discovered her errant daughter had up and left me." Hearing it, even in a joking manner caused Arabella to nestle even closer into his embrace.

"What did she say?" Arabella didn't know if she wanted to hear this or not.

"She told me where you were, what you were feeling and then she told me that we were going to have a baby."

Arabella's eyes widened and she instantly searched his face for insight into how he felt about this additional life that would be his responsibility. "We're having a baby?"

"You had no idea?"

"No. My thoughts have been so full of you, I haven't noticed anything else."

"If you remember, we made love several times without protection and I guess that one of those times we made a baby."

"How do you feel about this?" She watched his face carefully.

"I want a girl, a little girl with dark hair and eyes that shine like stars. I want a little girl who can work her magic on me and twist me around her little finger, just like her mother can." She was secretly glad he wanted a girl, because, as far as she knew, no female in her bloodline had ever had anything else.

"Thank you, Jade, for wanting us." Arabella was already including the baby in the equation. "I will love this baby with my whole heart and will treasure it the rest of my life – but there is one thing that you can be assured of ." She placed her hand on his face and looked deeply into his eyes. "It is you that I love more than life itself, it is you that I will cherish for the rest of my days. Forever, I will be grateful to the Wishing Moon for bringing you to me. You, my sweetheart, made my wish come true."

☾* ~ About the Author ~ *☽

Josie Arlington is the wife of a sweet conservative man, and the mother of a gorgeous 21 year old son who looks like a young Elvis Presley. She is also mother of one brilliant dachshund and 11 assorted felines.

Her love of reading romance is only surpassed by her love of writing. She lives in Texas and has roots in New Orleans.

****
COMING SOON!
****
MORE MOON MAGICK
Watch for Evangeline's story in "A Crescent Moon"

Check out her website at
www.josiearlington.com
for information on other projects.

WATCH THE WEBSITE FOR
♂ ~ *SPECIALTY ITEMS* ~ ♀
FEATURED IN EACH BOOK

BE SURE TO CHECK OUT OTHER SERIES BY JOSIE ARLINGTON

☾* ~ *MOON MAGICK SERIES*~ *☽
<u>Coming soon!</u>
A CRESCENT MOON
A BLUE MOON

♂ ~ *REDLAND ROUNDERS SERIES*~ ♀
T-R-O-U-B-L-E
<u>Coming soon!</u>
MY ALIYAH
SPANISH EYES

♥ ~ *SINFULLY SEXY SERIES*~ ♥
UNCHAINED MELODY
<u>Coming soon!</u>
FEVER
DON'T BE CRUEL

Made in the USA
Charleston, SC
18 January 2011